Sciron

David Rashleigh

ISBN: 978-0-9573671-0-4

Prologue

April 1941

In the docker's pub on Watery Lane, two men conversed in a corner of the smoky public bar. The younger man sipped his appropriately watery beer, occasionally glancing nervously at the other customers. His companion, sat with his back to the wall, spoke in hushed tones.

"We have a mission for you. An attack is planned against us. You and your associates are to help prevent it."

"'Course we will. What's the job?"

The older man explained for a few minutes, then glanced at the small suitcase by his side. "I have some small charges for you. A ship is due into Preston Dock tomorrow; the SS Orestes. She is coming to collect a cargo of munitions that are to be used against us. We want you to see that these munitions do not reach their destination."

"We'll never get near the ship" said the younger man. "And I don't suppose those firecrackers of yours will make much of a dent in her anyway."

"What do you suggest?"

"Are munitions coming by..." he broke off as an inebriated seaman stumbled past them. "Are they coming by rail?"

"We assume so. It is a cargo of rifle and artillery ammunition, grenades and so on. They are coming from the ordnance factory near Chorley, according to our sources."

"Well then. There's only one rail line down on to the dock. We'll just have to take it out of service for a while."

***

"See you in the morning, Dot." Jack Rimmer kissed his wife on the forehead and patted her swollen belly. Tin sandwich box in one hand, he slung his gas mask over his shoulder, picked up his flashlight and strode out of their red-brick terraced house. Another lonely night in the signal box beckoned: eight hours of quiet solitude occasionally punctured by the rattle of a passing train and the strident insistence of the bell that passed information to and from his neighbouring signalmen.

Born at the twilight of the Victorian era, Jack's youth had spared him from the carnage in Flanders that had taken his elder brother and two cousins. Now his age, and reserved occupation, kept him out of the current conflict. Marriage and impending fatherhood had come late to him: a career on the West Lancashire railway working shifts, coupled with a natural shyness, had not been conducive to socialising with the fairer sex. Having been employed in signal boxes serving the small villages between his native Southport and Preston had not helped, either. Two years earlier, following another move, this time to the north-easternmost box on the line at Penwortham Junction, he had married Dorothy Sellers who, now twenty-seven, was fourteen years his junior.

The shower-damp grass clung to Jack's boots as he climbed the railway embankment next to the fire station on Leyland Road, taking his habitual short-cut to work. As he crossed the wide bridge carrying the railway over Stricklands Lane, he thought, with some trepidation, about how life in their two up, two down home would change when their child was born. After all, what did he know about being a father? His life revolved around being a signalman, where virtually every eventuality was covered in the Rule Book. Jack was concerned that he may have left it too late:

4

after all, his father had been a young man, only twenty-two, when Jack was born.

He was still contemplating parenthood as he passed the small, brick-built privy and climbed the steps to the signal box.

"Evening, George" he called. "How's..." he broke off when he spied their Inspector standing at the opposite end of the row of painted levers. "Good evening, Mr Richards. To what do we owe this pleasure?"

"You'll find out soon enough, Jack. I need to speak to you. Hurry and change shift, you two."

The formalities completed, Jack and Richards were left alone in the signal box.

"There's a special train tonight, Jack." Richards was a large man, and was sweating in the warmth of the small room. He mopped his brow with a handkerchief and continued. "Did you hear what happened earlier? Some bastard blew up the dock railway, that's what. Set bombs under the track and on the tunnel portal. The track's fixed easy enough, but the tunnel isn't safe. There'll be nothing moving down there for the best part of a week."

"So how does that affect us?" asked Jack.

"There's a munitions train leaving the Royal Ordnance factory at Euxton tonight. It was due to go straight to the docks, but now it's coming our way. Set him back into the old station to unload then send him back to Euxton."

***

"We need to finish the job."

Three men in their late teens and early twenties were sat on the south bank of the river Ribble. Two were smoking, partly from the adrenaline that still coursed through their veins and partly to hide the stench of the low-tide mud.

"But we did for the tunnel mouth!" protested the non-smoker. "That line'll be shut for a month!"

"They've found another way around" said the first man. "Truckloads of squaddies from Weeton barracks are coming to move the munitions by hand. The train's going into the old station at the bottom of Fishergate hill."

"We used all the charges. How are we going to stop it?"

The third man pitched his cigarette end toward the slack water. A shower of sparks pierced the gathering gloom as it ricocheted off a small rock and disappeared with a gentle hiss. "We'll have to derail it. Somewhere where it'll stop any more getting through: one of the bridges on the Penwortham Triangle should do the trick."

***

Jack sat in the semi-darkness of the signal box; his chair faced the railway with the serried row of sixteen painted levers stood vertically before him. His fire spluttered and crackled, warming the twenty feet by twelve feet structure despite the pitiful amount of low-grade coal that constituted their meagre ration. The last scheduled train had passed; the dim red glow of its tail lamp heralding the solitude of the small hours that had been Jack's regular companion for much of his adult life. He allowed his eyes to scan the shelf of instruments in front of him: all appeared to be in order. Apart from one. Where there should have been a yellow glow in one of the matchbox-shaped indicators above the yellow lever at the right-hand end of the frame, there was nothing.

"Bugger!" thought Jack. The indicator told him that the lamp in one of his furthest signals had gone out: without it he would be unable to "give the road" to Whitehouse West signal box, and the munitions train would be delayed. This was an increasingly common problem. With so many people called up for military service, the lampmen who ensured that the paraffin in the lamps was topped up regularly were visiting less often, leading to the lamps simply running out. Several times recently, Jack had been forced to climb the signal post himself, fill and relight the lamp before returning to the signal box to allow a train to pass.

The signal in question was, fortunately, close not to Jack, but actually the other side of his colleague in Whitehouse West. A simple phone call would see the problem rectified within minutes. Jack lifted the handset of the direct line, to be met with silence in the earpiece.

Jack almost swore out loud. He tried other phones, he tried an emergency bell signal, but all means of communication were dead. The Rule Book didn't cover this one. Jack thought quickly. He realised that his only option was to walk the half mile or so to Whitehouse West, report the problem and relight his signal. He pulled on levers ten and eleven, setting the points to protect himself from an unscheduled train. Grabbing his flashlight, he left the comfort and security of his signal box and set off into the night.

The black, moonless night closed around him, punctured only by the beam of his flashlight. A sudden rustling noise startled him, and he shone his flashlight in the direction of the sound in time to see the tail of a large rat disappear down the embankment. Smiling grimly to himself, Jack continued, occasionally stumbling in the darkness and looking out for the faint yellow glimmering of Whitehouse West's twin distant signals. As the iron girders of the Stricklands Lane bridge became silhouetted against the stars, a movement, above the horizon, caught his eye. This time, it wasn't an animal. On the other side of the bridge, a man was clinging to the telegraph pole, one of a line that ran between the signal boxes carrying the phone lines and other electrical circuits.

"What are you doing up there?" shouted Jack, making his way across the short span. "Come down here, or I'll get the police!" There was another movement in front of him, and Jack shone his flashlight into the face of a man that stood before him with a yard-long platelayer's spanner held high in both hands. Jack felt the blood drain from his face with the shock of realisation. The man froze momentarily, opened his mouth to speak, then swung the spanner and Jack knew no more.

***

Sixty hours later, the ship that had been awaiting the munitions was making poor time. Despite the calm weather in the Bay of Biscay, they were barely making ten knots instead of the sixteen or so of which the ship was capable. The captain, a veteran of the previous world war, was regretting his decision to chase the convoy whose sailing they had missed after the delay in loading the munitions at Preston. He interrupted his pacing the bridge to speak to the chief engineer via the voice pipe.

"What's the hold up, Chief?" he asked for the third time in an hour. "We're a sitting duck at this speed!"

"I know, Sir." The laconic nature of the response was somehow accentuated by the heavy Welsh accent. "We've tried everything, but the fact remains that the boiler tubes are coked up. We need to blow them through, or we'll just get slower."

The captain already knew this, as he knew that the process of blowing tubes would create a huge pall of smoke that would mark their position to anybody within twenty miles.

"As soon as it gets dark. We daren't do it any sooner."

Their fate was already sealed. Less than two miles away, the ship was being observed intently. The entire twenty-two man crew of U145 were utterly silent, as they had been so many times before on their unsuccessful three-week mission. They had two torpedoes left, a result of having failed to sight any targets for them before returning to Lorient. The captain watched the ship through his periscope, passing fire control orders in a harsh whisper that reflected his barely-contained excitement.

On the bridge of the SS Orestes, a young lookout was scanning the sea's surface when he spotted the two tell-tale tracks heading straight for him.

"Captain! Torpedo tracks to starboard!" His Yorkshire accent failed to mask the panic in his voice, and he ran inside, grabbing a life preserver.

"Hard a-starboard!" shouted the captain to the wheelhouse. As the ship slowly, too slowly, began to turn, the captain knew that his vessel was doomed. Running back to the engine room voice pipe, he screamed once more at his engineers.

"Torpedoes! Get out of there, now, all of you!"

It was too late. Before a single stoker managed to reach the upper deck, one torpedo passed harmlessly ahead of the vertical prow of the ship. The second struck thirty feet back from the bow, five feet below the waterline, on the number two hold. That hold had been loaded at the ship's first port of call on the Clyde, where it had been filled with 250-pound bombs destined for the Blenheim light bombers of the RAF.

The sympathetic detonation simply vaporised the forward half of the ship. The remaining wreckage rolled over and sank within a few seconds, entombing forever the few men that had survived the initial explosion.

**

More than six decades later, an entirely different vessel was at work in the same waters. The MV Black Gold was a seismic survey vessel, hunting for reserves of oil and gas on the continental shelf that jutted into Biscay and was the prime cause of the rough seas for which the area is justly renowned. Unlike more modern vessels sporting powerful air guns, the Black Gold's marine geologist was forced to use half-pound explosive charges detonated forty feet below the surface. The resultant sound waves, bounced off the ocean floor, gave the scientists information as to the likelihood of oil or gas bearing strata.

The last charge had failed to go off, the result of a bad batch of fuses. The packet of explosives sank more than three hundred feet before settling on a man-made structure. The impact was sufficient to trigger the recalcitrant detonator, rupturing the metal surface on which it had come to rest and releasing a huge pocket of trapped air. The crew of the Black Gold saw the surface heave and burst upward, the ripples spreading outward, big enough to noticeably lift the rear of the vessel. Fearing that their trailing sensors may have been damaged, the Black Gold hove to while checks were made. It was during this hiatus that a crew member noticed something floating in the water where the eruption of air had been. A Gemini inflatable was lowered and sped toward the object. On arrival at the scene, the boat crew were shocked by the sight of a mummified corpse, floating in a kapok life preserver, dark holes where the eyes had once been and the mouth open in a perpetual silent scream.

April 2006

Monday

The town of Penwortham sits to the south of the river Ribble, opposite its larger and better-known neighbour, the city of Preston. From the air it vaguely resembles a fan held pointing south-west, one straight side formed by the river and the other bounded by the West Coast main railway line. Ancient thoroughfares to Liverpool and Wigan pass through, the latter running first south-eastward alongside the river, then turning south and shadowing the railway. This Leyland Road winds its way between late Victorian houses of varying sizes at river level before climbing the side of the river valley to what the locals call Pear Tree Brow after the pub close to the summit. On the left of a traveller leaving Preston, streets of smaller terraced houses form a triangle as the river curves first south, then away to the east. A few of these short, dead-ended roads delight in being ironically termed "Avenues", conjuring notions of shady, tree-lined boulevards, whilst in reality a thin veneer of tarmac covers the original cobbles and trees are notable only by their absence. Named after birds, such as Wren, Lark and Swallow, these narrow dead-end roads are frequently cluttered with cars that, when the houses were built, were as rare as private jets are today. To the right, the former homes of the nineteenth-century middle classes, some terraced, some semi- and a few detached, back onto an artificial embankment constructed in the early 1880's to carry trains directly from Blackburn to the West Lancashire railway's station at the bottom of Fishergate Hill, across the river.

Opposite Dove Avenue is Stricklands Lane, which, like the main road, climbs the side of the river valley and once ended in the grounds of Penwortham Hall. Crossed by the same railway that forms the backdrop to Leyland Road, the bridge was a wide steel lattice structure constructed to take two diverging lines and forming a point of what was known as the Penwortham Triangle. In the early twenty-first century, a developer had seen the potential for selling hard-core to the ever-hungry road industry whilst enabling him to make a tidy profit by building on the resultant land. This had entailed the excavation of the wide former railway embankment to the east of Stricklands Lane that had been dormant for nearly forty years, and had created a "brown field" site with sufficient land for a mini-estate of flats and small houses grouped into one cul-de-sac unimaginatively called The Junction.

***

Returning from her regular afternoon shift, Katie Melling pushed open the door of the second-floor flat at the entrance to The Junction that she shared with her husband and their son. Joshua was nearly two years old and quite a handful for the again-pregnant Katie. Her part-time job in the nearby Spar shop acted not only as an essential part of their income, but also gave her a break from Joshua's incessant energy. The climb to the flat left her increasingly tired; as she approached the door she braced herself for the whirlwind of exuberance that she knew would greet her.

"Mummy!" Joshua launched himself at Katie before she had time to close the door behind her.

"How's my little man?" Katie picked him up and was rewarded with an enthusiastic hug. "Have you been a good boy for Grandma?"

"Little angel, as always." Katie's mother called from the kitchen. Katie awaited the inevitable litany.

"You should let me do more to help" said her mother for the third time in a week. "And you should be looking for a bigger place to live."

"I know, Mum, but we can't afford to move. We can barely afford this place as it is. Besides, it may not be a great view, but it's a good area and we'll get the little ones into good schools from here."

The view that she referred to was the top of a huge sand-coloured stone wall, built over a hundred years previously as a bridge abutment. Above the wall, mature trees blotted out the sun in the summer; in the winter the west-facing aspect ensured that the sun was below the horizon before it could penetrate their home. The Melling's flat was almost at the level of the old railway line: anybody below their level had no view at all.

The flat was small but functional. Katie had had misgivings about moving in: something about it just didn't feel right. However, it was the best that they could afford, and her husband, Steve, had persuaded her that she was being irrational. Still, she occasionally had the feeling, when alone, that there was somebody in the flat with her.

"I'm off" called her mother as she tugged on the front door. "See you tomorrow."

"'Bye, Mum" Katie replied, putting Joshua down and walking into the compact living room. Joshua followed her. "Man!" he shouted, pointing out of the window at the abutment opposite. Katie, who had been in the process of sitting down, looked round but, despite sensing a slight movement, saw nobody.

"No, Josh, no man. Where's your book. I'll read to you." Katie was still looking across the lane.

"Man gone" burbled Joshua, and toddled off to fetch his Spot the Dog book.

Steve Melling returned home that evening, his hands grimy from labouring for a local landscape gardener. He followed his usual routine: a hug for his son, a kiss for his wife and a beer for himself. Two hours later, with their evening meal finished and their son put to bed, Steve and Katie exchanged small talk in front of the television. Katie stood up to close the curtains and was surprised by a torch shining through the trees across the road.

"Steve, there's somebody over there. I can see a torch being waved."

"It'll just be kids. Let me take a look." He pulled himself out of the chair and went to the window. "Must've gone. I can't see anyone."

"But I saw the torch! I've never seen anyone up there before."

"Like I said, it'll just be kids mucking about. Close the curtains and come and sit down."

"Josh saw somebody over there earlier. Said it was a man, not kids."

"Anyone over the age of ten is a man to him, Katie. Are you getting those funny feelings of yours again?"

"If you must ask, yes, I am" said Katie, taking one last look out of the window before returning to the sofa and curling up next to Steve.

***

On the opposite side of the Pennines, Mike Simpson was engaged in his eighth gun battle of the evening. At twenty-four years of age, he was a month or so younger than Katie Melling, but unlike her was unattached and lived at home in the Acomb area of York with his mother. Tall, with stooped shoulders covered in lank blonde hair, his face was scarred by the acne that still pockmarked his face. His mother despaired of him: she was sure that he should be out meeting girls instead of spending every evening in his room playing games. From his schooldays, Mike had always struggled with the opposite sex. The girls that were the object of his unrequited passion were never interested in him, preferring instead the boys with the right clothes, the right hair and the right line in chat. Many of those same girls were now pushing prams or taking their children to the same school that he had attended, whilst Mike's few sexual encounters had been disappointing and short.

Never having had a clear ambition in life, Mike had delighted his mother when, coming home from yet another course at the College of Further Education, he had announced that he had landed a job as a barrister. Her happiness had been short-lived: far from the high-powered career that she envisaged, it transpired that the position was not with a legal firm, but the city centre branch of a chain of coffee houses. He would not be defending the innocent or prosecuting the guilty, as a *barista* he would be serving them equally with espresso or latte.

Having acquired gainful employment, Mike had set about creating his own world. His first purchase had been a computer and a broadband connection to service it. That had led to his virtual incarceration in his bedroom every night as he tried first pornography, which he found unfulfilling and repetitive, than internet chatrooms. What had put the seal on his social life, however, was the advent of internet gaming via the Xbox 360. Now, whenever his shift was finished, he ceased to be plain Mike Simpson, and became instead "stealth_fighter", a virtual hero in cyberspace, where he was judged not by his sexual prowess, but by the number of headshots that he could achieve against his online enemies.

The long hours spent sat in a darkened room were beginning to impinge on his daytime activities. In quiet periods during the routine of the coffee house, he found himself daydreaming, re-enacting the battles of the previous night using the customers that he served as enemies, or saving them from imaginary terrorists with a single well-aimed shot. His lack of application to his real duties was becoming more apparent to his co-workers, and he had been warned by the manager more than once about his lassitude.

Tonight, though, none of that mattered. He had just shot the fifteenth opponent in the ten-minute contest without suffering a virtual death himself. As he was lining up on his next victim, his senses were assaulted by the sudden manifestation of an overpowering smell of dampness, accompanied by a feeling of intense hatred, palpable but seemingly not directed at himself.

Freezing momentarily, he was sufficiently distracted not to notice that not only had his intended victim escaped, but had managed to shoot him instead. Fleetingly, Mike sensed a movement behind him. Snapping his head around, eyes wide with apprehension, he was relieved to see nothing except his bed. A moment later, the room had returned to normal; the smell, the feeling having disappeared as quickly as they came. Mike returned to his game but, now distracted, he was easy meat for his opponents and so logged off and gave up at the relatively early hour of eleven thirty.

***

Later that night, Katie awoke. Blearily she struggled to focus on the clock. Its pale green glow told her that it was half past three, while the sound of Joshua's voice made her comprehend why she had woken up. With Steve sound asleep, and not snoring for once, she swung her legs out of the bed and padded softly to her son's bedroom. She paused at the door and listened. It sounded like Joshua was talking to somebody; at least as much as a toddler can hold a conversation.

She gently pushed the door open. Joshua was stood up in his cot facing away from her.

"Who are you talking to, Joshie?" she asked. The little boy turned to face her, startled at the sound of her voice. The momentary fright made him start to cry, and Katie plucked him from his bed and held him to her.

"Now then, it's only me. No need to cry." Her voice quickly soothed him. "Who were you talking to?" she asked again.

"Man" replied Joshua.

An uneasy feeling washed over Katie. "There's no man here. Daddy's in bed, asleep."

Joshua looked toward the corner of his bedroom opposite the door.

"Man gone" he said, cuddled up to his mother, and quickly fell asleep. Katie gently placed him in his cot and returned to her bedroom. She toyed with the idea of waking Steve, but, knowing how uncommunicative he could be when woken in the small hours, elected instead to speak to him over breakfast. She lay awake for another hour, trying to rationalise her deep disquiet. Her discomfiture was not helped by her unborn child, who chose that moment to kick and writhe within her extended abdomen. The attempt at making sense of her fears was fruitless, and she knew that her husband was unlikely to understand.

Tuesday

As she expected, Steve was dismissive of Katie's worries. Looking into her hazel eyes, he gently cradled her cheek in his rough, calloused hand.

"There was no man, love. He was probably still dreaming, or sleepwalking, or something. Now, I'll be late if I don't get going." He pulled on the dirty fleece that served as a work coat and grabbed his keys from the hook beside the door. Pausing in the doorway, he turned to her and smiled. "You'll be fine. Say hello to the battleaxe for me."

Katie returned his smile, but without enthusiasm. She knew that he was right, of course. There was no man, was there? Whilst nobody had ever called him a genius, Steve was the rational one, the practical one, who worked every hour possible to pay the rent on the flat and the other bills that seemed to get bigger almost every month. She smiled again to herself, this time a genuine expression of contentment, and went to dress their little boy.

Outside, in the spring sunshine, Steve's progress along the narrow pavement was blocked by a straight-backed, grey-haired man in his mid-sixties who was staring up at the embankment opposite their flat. He seemed quite unaware of Steve's presence. Steve followed the man's gaze but saw nothing out of the ordinary.

"Excuse me, chief" said Steve, using his habitual term for a stranger.

The man started out of his reverie. "Sorry," he said, and stepped to one side. Steve smiled his thanks and headed toward his day's labours.

Half an hour later, Katie struggled down the stairs with Joshua's buggy, Joshua himself following behind with the one-step-at-a-time gait of a child carefully descending. As Katie opened the front door of the building, he ran outside, straight into the legs of the man that had unintentionally obstructed his father. The man stumbled backwards, lost his footing on the kerb and fell into the road, twisting and striking his forehead on the tarmac. He lay still for a moment, and Katie feared that he had been knocked unconscious. Joshua stood, his blue eyes like saucers, until his mother caught up with him. He clung to her leg, preventing her from helping as the man stirred and groggily got to his feet. He looked at Katie, who saw a trickle of blood run down the man's face and drip off the end of his nose.

"I'm terribly sorry!" gasped Katie. "Are you all right?"

"I...think so," said the man as he hesitantly regained the footpath. "I may need to sit down for a few minutes, though."

"Please, come inside" said Katie. It's a couple of flights of stairs, but at least I can clean up that cut."

"Thank you. You are most kind. But aren't you going somewhere?"

"Only shopping. It can wait."

The three of them slowly made their way back up the stairs, pausing frequently. Entering the flat, Joshua headed for his toys whilst the out-of-breath Katie and the unsteady man went into the kitchen. As she tended his wound, Katie apologised once more for her son's impetuosity.

"No need," said the man. "I should introduce myself. My name's Jack. Jack Rimmer. Here." He handed over a business card.

Katie completed the introductions. "I've not seen you around before, have I?"

"Probably not," replied Jack. "But I am from around here originally." He went on to explain that he had been born nearby,

19

had grown up and gone to school all in that locality. On leaving school, however, he had joined the army and returned only occasionally to visit his mother. Since her funeral, some thirty-two years earlier, he had not been back. He had retired from the army after the first Gulf War, at the age of fifty, and had made his living since writing history books for specialist publishing houses.

"Things must have changed a bit since you were last here. What made you come back now?" inquired Katie.

"I'm actually researching my father," said Jack. "Mother told me that he died before I was born, and I know very little about him. It's a sort of voyage of discovery, if you like, set off by finding a few documents in an old biscuit tin from my mother's house. What I do know is that he worked on the railway that used to pass through here."

"What railway?" Katie had no idea what the stone wall across the road was.

"Didn't you know? That wall opposite is one half of the bridge that carried the railway. Your flat was built where another embankment used to be. You can see the continuation of it opposite the fire station. You know, next to the church. It's a footpath now. I only have one photo of my father. Would you like to see it?" Katie nodded.

He reached into his jacket pocket and pulled out a slightly crumpled black and white photograph of a bride and groom and showed it to Katie. Joshua wandered over and looked at the photograph. Smiling up at Katie, he pointed at the bridegroom.

"Man!"

***

Jack Rimmer sat in the uncomfortable armchair that filled far too much of the space in his hotel room, deep in thought. As an historian, he was used to puzzles, fitting together the pieces of somebody's life or a long-forgotten battle. This was different, personal. His objectivity, essential to producing a balanced history book, might be sorely tested.

Unable to get comfortable in the chair and nursing a headache from his fall, Jack left the efficient but soulless motel and headed for the pub next door. Installing himself at a corner table with a large glass of house red, he surveyed the sparse Tuesday night clientele. Concluding that he was unlikely to be disturbed, he allowed his thoughts to return to the scarcity of information in his possession. It had been a chance discovery, an old Peak Frean's biscuit tin tucked away in his attic, covered in dust and the droppings of a long-dead bird that had found itself trapped beneath Jack's roof. It had evidently formed his father's filing system: it contained, among the assorted trivia, a collection of payslips and the letter appointing him to his last position as signalman at Penwortham Junction signal box.

Jack pondered his next move. He had already ordered his father's birth certificate and it was probably sat on the hall carpet at his house in a suburb of Ashford. For some reason, he had been unable to find any reference to his father's death certificate, which was unusual to say the least. The purpose of his visit to Preston had been to trawl the local archives, but, apart from some old maps and some history of the West Lancashire railway, his efforts had been frustrated. He had to return home soon, since his modest success as an author did not allow for extended stays in hotels, and he wanted to dig deeper into the mystery of the elder Jack's demise. A phone call to the National Railway Museum in York had determined that their library was closed for refurbishment, so there was little point in crossing the Pennines for background information. Jack drained his glass and returned to his room to pack.

***

There was a fault at the local telephone exchange, meaning that Mike's broadband connection was down. Unable to bring himself to leave the sanctuary of his bedroom, he decided instead to reacquaint himself with the music collection left behind by his father. Comprising largely of rock music of the late sixties and early seventies, his discovery that he preferred it to more modern renditions served to accentuate his inability to fit in with his peers. Lying on his bed, the shape of his head distorted by the bulky headphones that he wore to avoid his mother's wrath, Mike was listening to a live album by Eric Clapton. The lights were off, and the music sufficiently loud that the rest of the world was blocked out. Mike's eyes were closed; mental images of himself standing on the stage of the Albert Hall, a cherry red Gibson ES335 in hand, played across his mind as once again he replaced reality with fantasy. He barely noticed the growing odour of salt water, the virtual clamminess in the atmosphere or the emerging sense of loathing that permeated his surroundings: he was concentrating on his imaginary audience, another riff from his air guitar bringing them to their feet in a fantasy frenzy of adulation. Nor did he, at first, register the voice that infested the lyrics.

"In the white room..."

You must help me

"...with black curtains..."

It's dark...so cold

"...by the station."

He did this to us

"Black-roof country..."

He must atone for what he did

"...no gold pavements..."

He killed us

"...tired starlings."

BRING HIM TO US!

The last sentence finally penetrated Mike's consciousness. His unreal audience had been replaced with a fleeting vision of a man, dripping water and staring at him. He sat bolt upright, sweat bursting from his brow and a sense of panic gripping him. His mother burst into the room, ran to the bed and shook him by his shoulders. Mike suddenly realised that he had been shouting out loud and looked pleadingly into his mother's eyes. She, in turn, removed his headphones and sat next to him, her arm around him.

"What's the matter, love?" she managed to keep the concern in her voice to a minimum.

"I...I don't know. Th..th..there was a man...he was talking to me."

"There's nobody here. You must have been dreaming. You really shouldn't spend all this time up here on your own, it's not good for you."

"But Mum, I wasn't asleep...at least, I don't think I was...no. I can't have been. The voice was mixed in with the music."

"They would be, if the music was still on when you were asleep. Come on, come downstairs and have a drink. It was just a dream, and you'll be fine in a moment." She managed to keep the note of triumph out of her voice: her nagging that he spent too much time alone was finally vindicated.

Mike acquiesced, and gingerly followed her down the stairs, still reeling at his experience. If only he could remember what was said...

Wednesday

Katie was dozing. The leaden sky, and the unseasonably heavy downpour that emanated from it, combined with the trees opposite to cast a deep gloom over the living room. Wednesday was her day off; her Steve was working and little Joshua was having his afternoon nap. After an hour's ironing, she had curled up on the sofa with her head languishing on the arm and her long hair cascading into an auburn waterfall. The rhythmic pulsing of the rain on the window had an almost hypnotic cadence, causing her mind to meander through that trance-like state where the boundaries between dream and reality blur and intertwine. A dejected whisper, barely audible, seemed to penetrate her consciousness.

Dorothy....I'm lost, Dorothy...help me....

Katie was dimly aware of a figure standing over her. She sensed a deep sadness.

Dorothy...I can't find my way home...where are you, my love...the baby...

At that, Katie's eyes snapped open. She was alone in the room, but a visceral melancholia remained. In her post-waking confusion, she battled against a rising fear with the conviction that the recent occurrences had manifested themselves as a dream. Dazedly rising to her feet, guided by her maternal instinct, she checked on her still-slumbering boy. Having satisfied herself that all was well, she turned to make for the kitchen and shrieked with fright at the figure of a man stood in front of her.

"Jesus, Steve! You frightened the life out of me!" Her husband grinned and threw his arms around her.

"What's up, love? Aren't you pleased to see me?"

"I just didn't hear you come in, that's all. You're early?" She returned his hug, half turning as her baby kicked within her.

"It's raining too hard. We can't get anything done. How about a brew?"

"You make us one. I need to sit down." Despite the continuing deluge, the atmosphere in the living room had lightened markedly. Katie sat, still troubled by her dream. A few minutes later, Steve sat next to her, handing over a steaming mug of tea.

"I'm beginning to worry about you," he said, frowning. "You still look like you've seen a ghost."

"Just a dream, that's all. I fell asleep before and dreamt that someone was whispering to me. It wasn't the whispering, it was the voice. It was just so...sad. And it mentioned a baby. That's when I woke up: at least, I think I woke up. It was all so real, I really can't tell."

"Of course it was just a dream, love," said Steve dismissively. "It's just the baby talking."

"How would you know!" snapped Katie, a rising anger causing her voice to break. "I feel like somebody is watching me, Josh thinks he's been talking to a man that's been dead for years and all you can do is say that it was just a dream!" Tears were welling in her eyes as a plaintive cry from the little bedroom broke the tension between them.

"I'll see to him" said Steve, realising that a hasty retreat was his best course of action. He smiled sympathetically at Katie and went to attend to Joshua.

***

The drive back to Ashford had been a six-hour nightmare. Despite frequent stops and the comfortable seats in his ageing Honda Accord, Jack Rimmer's back was sheer agony and his legs were numb. Another band of heavy rain had caused two accidents on the M6, delaying Jack's arrival on the London orbital motorway until the evening rush. Welcome to the M25, Jack had thought, grimly, the world's biggest car park. His house felt cold, so Jack sat at the kitchen table with a mug of coffee while he worked his way through the pile of mail that had partially obstructed his front door. Dropping the junk mail straight into the recycling bin that he kept by the back door, he worked his way through his latest gas bill and a letter from his publisher before opening the buff envelope from the Family Records Centre.

The red and cream certificate was in itself a mine of information: it informed Jack that his paternal grandfather, William Rimmer, had been a groundsman, and that his wife's maiden name had been Geraldine Roberts. Jack racked his brain for memories of his grandparents; fleeting images of a kindly but sad old man were overwhelmed by intrusive recollections of his mother's occasional bitterness at having to raise a child without a father. His father's date of birth, on the fourth of January 1901, was another useful clue: he should appear on the census of that year that was freely available via the internet.

The house having warmed a little, Jack moved into the former dining room that he used as a study, fired up his laptop and connected to his favourite genealogy site. A few moments searching was sufficient to find the entry he sought: William Rimmer, his wife Geraldine and their sons...sons? He had an uncle? According to the census page, there were two children in the Rimmer household. Jack, aged three months, and Albert, aged four years. Looking at the relative ages of the family, it was clear that William and Geraldine had become parents in their late teens, and that Albert would have been of military age during the First World War. A brief search of the Commonwealth War Graves Commission website gave one A W Rimmer, a private with the King's Liverpool Regiment, who had been killed during the Allied offensive at the Ypres Salient on the thirty-first of July 1917.

Jack paused and sat back in his chair, his chin resting on his steepled fingers. Although he clearly had no proof yet that this was his uncle, he had mixed emotions about this discovery. Having researched war casualties before, he knew that behind each stark statistic was a grieving family, a father, son or brother that would never return to their loved ones. This one may be different, however. This time, his own father may have been the brother, aged just sixteen, trying to cope with his own grief while acutely aware that his parents' life had just been rent asunder.

With some difficulty, Jack put his thoughts aside and contemplated how he could discover what had happened to his father. His mother had been adamant; he had died before Jack was born and had deflected any enquiry regarding what actually happened to him. Yet there was no death certificate, and no grave that he knew of. His only clue was the time frame: the nine-month span of his own gestation! Jack quickly realised that he would have to make another trip to Preston, this time to search the back issues of the local newspaper, the Lancashire Evening Post. More in hope than expectation, he logged on to the Public Record Office website and put a few keywords into their search engine. To his surprise, the words "Rimmer, West Lancashire railway, 1941" resulted in a hit on the catalogue. His curiosity pricked, he clicked on the obscure file reference. He was amused to read the summary of its contents: a Security Service report into somebody, or something, called "Sciron". Since his father had been a railway signalman, this obviously had nothing to do with his current research. The codename intrigued him: perhaps this would give him an idea for his next book. Indeed, the public records office at Kew was far closer to home, and this would give him an excuse not to head back to Lancashire for another day. Jack looked at his watch and was surprised to see that it was past midnight. Suddenly tired, he pre-ordered the file to be readied for his visit, shut down his computer and turned in for the night.

***

Mike was in a foul mood. Lack of sleep had meant that he had been upbraided by his manager at work yet again, but his sense of injustice had been magnified by his mother, who, emboldened by Mike's behaviour the night before, had announced that henceforth his board and lodging would no longer be free of charge. This unwelcome fragment of reality, and the brief but heated and utterly indefensible argument that had followed, had distracted him sufficiently to have induced a particularly poor performance when he had finally adopted his now restored online persona. Shaking with rage, he had actually thrown the controller across his bedroom when he lost the eighth consecutive game.

He now lay on his bed, hands behind his head, staring at the ceiling and rehearsing in his mind the crushing put-downs that he would deliver to his persecutors in the morning. Of course, he would never actually have the courage to go through with it: he would meekly apologise to his mother over breakfast and turn up at work, on time and without a word. This knowledge served only to intensify his anger and frustration, which consumed his attention so completely that he didn't notice that there was, once again, a growing odour of the seaside. When the realisation finally dawned on him, Mike was also aware that his own emotions had been overwhelmed by the sense of hatred that he had felt the previous two nights. Sitting up, his peripheral vision caught the outline of a man bathed in the glow from the television. Snapping his head to the right, he caught only a fleeting glimpse of the shadowy figure as it vanished through his bedroom door, the other assaults on his senses and emotions fading as quickly as they had arisen.

Jumping to his feet, Mike pulled open the door and looked out on to the landing. To his right, the bathroom door was ajar as usual; to his left, his mother's bedroom emanated the sound of gentle snoring. Moving to the top of the stairs, he looked over the banister into the darkness below, but there was no sign of his intruder. Now shaken by his experience, his hands were trembling uncontrollably. His first thought was to go to his mother, although whether it was for her protection or his own comfort he really couldn't be sure. After a moment's indecision, his fear had subsided sufficiently for him to gather his wits and return to his own room, where he lay, sleepless and fidgeting, until the first glimmerings of dawn filtered into his room.

The tired meanderings of his mind dragged up a memory from his childhood. His mother, tears streaming down her face, pleading with his father not to walk out on them whilst accusing him of giving up the moment that life got difficult. He had no way of knowing that the difficulty in question had been the buxom barmaid from the pub that had been his father's second home, but he remembered his mother's words clearly.

"You always do this! You just give up! Call yourself a man? A real man would face his problems, not run away!"

Mike decided, at that point, that he would face up to whatever it was that had started to, well, haunt him. With that realisation, a shiver ran down his spine, and he wondered how long this new-found resolve would last. He would find out, soon enough.

Thursday

Katie looked at the bedside clock. It was ten past three in the morning, and she was being kept awake by the snoring of her husband and the unrelenting wriggling of her unborn baby. Try as she might, she could not get comfortable: if she lay on her side, the baby kicked all the more; lying on her back felt as unnatural to her as it always had. Giving Steve one more unsuccessful nudge, she gave up the unequal struggle and went to get a drink. Passing by Joshua's bedroom, she listened at the door. Reassured by the sound of his breathing, she continued into the kitchen. Filling the kettle, she was once again aware of a despondent atmosphere surrounding her, filling the kitchen. As the kettle began its gentle hiss, Katie's mind was assailed by a sensation of sheer misery; as if a terrible event had occurred that was locked in the deepest recesses of her memory. Yet she had experienced no such trauma throughout her uneventful life. As the sound from the kettle grew louder, the memory of the previous afternoon reasserted itself and the same unhappy whispering projected itself onto her consciousness.

Dorothy...is that you? He hit me, Dot...why did he hit me?

The kettle reached a crescendo, but still the voice penetrated the roar of boiling water.

Dorothy, turn around, love. I'm hurt. Help me...please.

Katie froze. She sensed a presence behind her, and her fear made her blood run cold. As if sensing danger, the baby was still. Her legs were like jelly, and her hands trembled as she steadied herself against the worktop. There was a loud click, and the sound from the kettle rapidly diminished. The whispering had stopped, but the mood remained. Katie steadied herself, taking a deep breath and swallowing hard. Silence reigned. Regaining some of her composure, she reached up and took a mug from the cupboard above the kettle. Tea bags were in the caddy next to her, and she poured the steaming water over the pyramid-shaped bag. Moving to her left, she bent to open the fridge for the milk. Having grasped the bottle, a sudden cramp in her back made her straighten up rapidly, leaving her facing the uncurtained kitchen window. Reflected in the glass was the outline of a man, standing behind her.

"Steve," she said, turning. "What are you...."

It was not her husband. The man before her was taller, but more slightly built. His face was gaunt and grey; his black eyes looked out from under heavy, drooping eyelids. His mouth was turned downward and his expression one of utter wretchedness. Looking quizzically at Katie, the man lifted his right hand, reaching out for her. The hand was a different colour to the face, and, despite her terror, Katie realised that the hand was covered with blood. Katie looked again at the man's face, and saw that the side of his head and his hair was also bloodstained. She felt her legs buckle beneath her, and the last thing that she heard was that same whisper.

Hello, Dot...I've found you at last.

Steve Melling was awakened by the sound of breaking glass. Not sure whether he had dreamed it, he turned to his wife only to find a cold space where she should have been. Suddenly concerned, he swung his legs out of the bed and pulled on his dressing gown. Leaving the bedroom, he stubbed his toe on the doorframe and swore out loud. Knowing that such language within earshot of their son would earn him a rebuke from his wife, the silence that greeted his outburst served to make him anxious about Katie.

Spotting that the kitchen light was on, Steve made his way across the small hallway that connected the five rooms of their flat. Entering the kitchen, he was shocked to find Katie sprawled across the floor, surrounded by broken glass and a pool of milk stained with blood from a gash on her leg. Carefully sweeping away the

31

shards of glass, Jack lifted his wife's head and cradled it on his knees.

"Katie, wake up! What happened, love?"

At the sound of his voice Katie stirred. Her eyelids flickered, and she looked up at Steve's face. Upon recognising him, she clung tightly to his arm and burst into tears. Steve had seen his wife crying before, but never like this. Sobs racked her body and it seemed that she was struggling for breath. Realising that the loss of half a pint of milk could not be the cause of such anguish, Steve looked around the compact kitchen for another reason. Everything was as it should be, including the steaming mug next to the kettle.

"Come on, sweetheart, let's sort you out." Steve helped Katie to her feet and led her into the living room. Sitting her down on the sofa, he returned to the kitchen for their small first aid kit. Having bandaged Katie's leg, he found her a clean nightie and helped her to change. Seeing that she was still too traumatised to speak and unable to think of anything to say to her, Steve went back into the kitchen and began to clear the mess on the floor.

He had cleaned up the broken glass and was mopping the floor tiles when he realised that Katie was standing in the doorway.

"How are you feeling?" Steve enquired.

Katie's voice was hollow. "There was a man here," she said, her head resting on the door frame. "His hand and the side of his head were covered in blood. He called me Dot, and said that he had found me."

"There can't have been anyone in here!" spluttered Steve. He gently pushed past his wife and checked that the door, the only way in or out of their home, was not only locked but securely bolted from the inside. A swift examination of the rest of the flat confirmed that all the windows were shut, too.

"He was here, Steve." Katie had not moved, and spoke over her shoulder. "He spoke to me. I didn't imagine it. It was real."

Steve came up behind her and put his arms around her middle, holding her close. Logic told him that it couldn't possibly be true, yet something in Katie's voice made him believe it.

"He called me Dot. He thinks that I'm somebody else."

A shiver ran down Steve's spine. The visions, the voices, either all were true or his wife was suffering some sort of breakdown. He found that he wanted to believe that their flat was haunted, since the alternative was too horrible to contemplate.

"It's all true, Steve. All of it." said Katie, as if she had read her husband's mind. "Joshua has seen him too, and spoken to him."

"But who is he? A ghost? How do you get a ghost in a brand new flat?" Steve was struggling with the concept, his mind blinkered by the traditional notion that ghosts only haunted old buildings.

Katie, remembering her conversation with Jack Rimmer, made the connection for him. "He isn't haunting this flat. He's haunting the old railway line."

***

Walking along the wide flagged pathway between the shallow ponds, Jack Rimmer was, as always, nonplussed by the Public Records Office building in front of him. A modern yet tasteful (Jack was no fan of the modern architect) glass-fronted entrance hall directly ahead of him was overshadowed by a grotesque concrete edifice to the left. Rows of narrow windows gave the structure the look of a giant layer cake. It was this part of the building; however, that Jack knew contained some of the most important historical documents in the world. The Domesday Book and Magna Carta were probably the most famous residents, two among millions of fascinating insights into the past.

Passing through the entrance, Jack signed in using his reader's ticket and proceeded left, between the gift shop and the restaurant, toward the security gate. Just before the gate, he turned right into the locker room. Here, he collected a clear plastic bag and placed his notebook and a couple of pencils in it. Returning to then security gate, he showed the bag to the guard who gave it a cursory examination before permitting Jack to scan his ticket and pass through the turnstile. Going up one flight of stairs, Jack turned left and, passing through another glass door into the reading room, turned left again and went to collect his pre-ordered file.

Having received the buff-coloured folder, he made for one of the tables in the reading room. Nods of recognition were passed between Jack and a number of regulars, many retired men and women who spent their time as amateur historians and who Jack knew from his past visits. Sitting down, he took his notebook from the bag and opened it to a clean page. Placing the folder in front of him, Jack looked at the cover. He was intrigued to see "Most Secret" stamped on the cover: this was an interesting document indeed. As he began to read the contents, it quickly became evident that "Sciron" was the codename of an agent operating in Britain during the Second World War and being hunted by MI5, whose file this had been until released under the thirty year rule. From the early part of the document, it wasn't clear who the agent worked for: he was believed to have been a Polish Jew and therefore working for the Soviet security service, the OGPU. He had been observed attending Trades Union meetings and consorting with known members of the Communist Party, thus reinforcing the conviction of his case officer that Sciron was a Soviet spy.

Jack perused the date-ordered pages, scanning through them until he reached the early part of 1941. Then he began to study them in more detail, wondering where the reference that had caused the hit from the search engine would fit in. Eventually, he came across a three-page typed report form a field operative dated May 1941. On reading it, Jack's jaw dropped. He tried to read it again, but, to his surprise, a feeling of loss permeated his mind and disrupted his concentration. Realising that he had not written a word in his notebook, and slightly ashamed that what he had read could affect him so deeply, he closed the folder and took a moment to regain his composure. Finally, still blinking back tears, he moved to the photocopying room at the far end of the reading area and copied the report. He then returned the file and made his way back down the stairs, his distracted state causing him to bump into more than one other researcher.

Over a cup of too-strong tea in the restaurant, Jack tried to make sense of what he had read. He scanned the document once again, still not daring to believe its contents. One thing he did believe, though, was the author of the report. The document was initialled CJM, which Jack recognised as Cedric Morgan, a former Security Service officer whom he had interviewed whilst researching an earlier commission. Prior to the war, Morgan had been a Classics scholar at Jesus College, Oxford, and was renowned for giving the subjects of his reports names from Greek mythology. Hence the name "Sciron", which meant nothing to Jack but undoubtedly had significance for the author. Unfortunately, Morgan's contact details were in Jack's study, back in Ashford. Cursing silently, Jack drained his tea and set off for home once again.

***

As Jack Rimmer was reversing out of the car park at Kew, Katie Melling was sat in her living room staring out of the window. Earlier that morning, having explained to her husband about the history of their home and its surroundings, she had persuaded him to go to work. He had reluctantly agreed, having extracted from his wife a promise that she would call in sick and ask her mother to look after Joshua. Her mother had been understandably concerned: Katie had convinced her that she was just tired after a sleepless night. Suitably mollified, she had taken her grandson to her house to allow her daughter to rest.

Rest, however, was not forthcoming. Katie could not settle at all. She had cleaned the flat, prepared the dinner, but whenever she tried to rest the memories came back to haunt her. It occurred to her that she had sensed no malice from the apparition, just the feeling of dejection. When he had reached out to her, she remembered, the movement had not been in the slightest menacing. She recalled Joshua's experience: if it was the same man, he was clearly no threat. Katie closed her eyes and tried to picture the scene from the early hours: the man, the blood...his clothes. He had been hatless, wearing a short jacket, waistcoat and dark trousers: in his other hand had been a torch.

But who was Dot? Katie surmised that she must be his wife; after all, the man had to be well over forty and so was probably married. But why did he think that Katie was his wife? Surely Dot must have been close to the same age? A sudden realisation dawned on her: Dot must have been pregnant. A shudder went down Katie's spine at the thought. Was that it? Did the apparition think that Katie was his wife? It would explain why he appeared to have latched on to Katie.

"Who are you?" Katie realised that she had spoken out loud. "What do you want with me? I'm not Dot."

Where's Dot?

The sudden whisper made Katie jump. "I don't know. I don't know who Dot is."

My wife...she's my wife. She's pregnant...I'm going to be a father... who are you?

"Katie. I may be pregnant, but I'm not your wife." Katie realised that she was less afraid than before, despite the slight tremor in her voice. She paused for a moment. "Who are you?"

I...I'm...Jack.

"Jack who?"

Jack...Rimmer. Where's Dot? I'm lost...can't find her, can't get home.

The intense sadness had returned. Unsure what to say next, Katie waited for a minute before risking a glance over her shoulder. Hesitantly, she turned her head but the terrifying spectre from the night before was nowhere to be seen. She breathed a sigh of relief; as she exhaled, she noticed a movement in the trees opposite. She glimpsed the outline of a tall man, his back to her and a torch in his hand, disappearing along the old embankment. As he vanished, so did the air of melancholy.

As the atmosphere returned to normal, Katie recalled the elderly man that had been felled by Joshua. His name had been Jack Rimmer, too.

Friday

The following evening, George Williams sat in the working men's club nursing a pint of bitter. Eighty-five years old, the drink that he sipped occasionally summed up his character perfectly. "Victor Meldrew without the laughs," as one wag had all-too-accurately described him. He had spent his working life as a railwayman and a union activist; the latter activity carried out with more enthusiasm than the former and both with a distinct lack of diplomacy. Having been persuaded by a grateful management to take early retirement some twenty-five years earlier, he had launched himself into a short-lived political career by standing for election to Preston council. Standing as a Socialist Worker candidate during the Falklands War, he polled fewer than a dozen votes in a well-to-do area in the north of the borough. Having been a fervent socialist since leaving school, he took his rejection by the electorate as a personal humiliation. The years since had been spent leading the solitary life of a single pensioner, his wife having finally grown tired of his one-dimensional conversation and left him for, of all people, a Tory councillor that she had met while learning Spanish at evening classes.

Now his days were filled by the Daily Mirror and the Labour club. It was here that he had built up a small following of what he liked to call "young firebrands" who, he thought, shared his view of the world and his dismay at the incumbent Labour government's failure to implement full-blooded socialism. As George took another sip of his beer, one of his coterie entered the club.

"Evenin', Grandad." The man, Kevin Anderson, was in his early thirties, thick-set, tattooed and shaven-headed. "Grandad" was an honorary title: George had never had children. Anderson was, simply put, a thug. Of slightly below average intelligence and, like so many of his generation, poorly educated, his favoured method of dispute resolution comprised a combination of anatomically impossible suggestions and his fists. This tendency meant that Anderson had never held down a full time job for more than a few months, his latest career usually ending with the broken nose of a fellow employee following some affront, real or imagined. He had a soft spot for the old man, though. He came over to join George, a pint of Stella Artois in one hand and a replacement pint for George in the other.

By ten that evening their regular group, five in all, were gathered around the same table putting the world to rights. The remaining three were a mixed bunch: a taxi driver, a lecturer at one of the local further education colleges and Steve Melling.

***

Two sleepless nights on Tuesday and Wednesday had meant that nothing could have prevented Mike Simpson from falling into a deep slumber as soon as he laid on his bed on his return from work on Thursday evening. He had, in fact, slept solidly for fourteen hours, still dressed in his work clothes. His mother, fussing as always, had thrown a blanket over him and left him to sleep. Consequently, on Friday evening, as the "comrades" were gathering in the Labour club, Mike still felt fresh. Out of habit, he switched on his game console and loaded the game. As the system connected to the internet, Mike paused. He realised that his head was full of anticipation of another visitation, and found himself occasionally sniffing the air to pick up the first hint of the olfactory revelation that would herald the return of...what? His new-found determination that had accompanied the dawn chorus of the morning before was suddenly less resolute, but even so he switched off the Xbox and sat, cross-legged, on his bed. His mother was in her bedroom, carefully applying makeup for her regular Friday night out: quite what she got up to Mike had no idea. He didn't always hear her come in...Mike shook his head and tried to dismiss the thought: the prospect of his mother actually having sex was simply too awful to contemplate. After all, she was, at forty-five, past all that...wasn't she? At that moment, as if sensing what he was thinking, she chose to magnify his discomfort by coming into his room. Wearing a black knee-length sleeveless dress with a plunging neckline and three-inch stilettos, Mike thought she looked ridiculous.

"I'm off now. Don't wait up" she said, winking suggestively.

"Oh, go on" replied Mike, really embarrassed now. "Behave yourself...please?"

Without replying, she smiled, then turned and disappeared down the stairs, leaving a trail of perfume lingering in her wake.

Mike waited for the front door to close, then went downstairs to raid the kitchen. Standing in front of the tall upright fridge, he held the door open as he scanned the contents. Eventually selecting a wedge of Wensleydale cheese, he returned to his room and began to nibble at it. Half an hour later, he was sitting in his chair, stereo blasting out Kashmir, when once again the sense of hatred enveloped him and the stench of the beach at low tide assaulted his nostrils.

Switching off the music, Mike steeled himself and turned towards the door. Framed in the doorway was the figure of a man, his short hair matted flat and rivulets of water running down his distorted face and on to what seemed to be overalls. Mike froze, unable to speak. The sheer menace that exuded from the apparition was overpowering, exacerbated by the spectre lifting one bony hand and pointing at him.

You must help me.

Mike's mouth just gaped.

He left me trapped. You must bring him to me.

"Wh...who? Bring who?" Mike was shaking uncontrollably now.

The man who killed us. The man who killed the signalman and condemned me to die, trapped, alone.

"I...I don't understand! Who is he? Why do you want me to bring him?"

You are the last in my line. You must bring him to us so that he can atone. I cannot rest until justice is done. Bring him to the Penwortham Triangle.

***

It was past ten thirty, and Katie Melling was curled up on the sofa in her living room. Jack would be back from the club in the next half hour, and she had not yet had an opportunity to tell him of that afternoon's experience. Next to her on the small table was a half empty mug of tea that had gone cold un-noticed. In her hand was Jack Rimmer's business card. Her mother had returned Joshua earlier in the evening; the little boy had had a bath and gone to bed three hours earlier. Katie had spent the intervening time wrestling with the decision whether to contact the elderly historian. If there was no link between him and the apparition, she would look foolish; on the other hand, the events of the past few days were preying on her mind. She was desperate for an answer, an explanation for what was happening to her and her family. Twice she had dialled the number and immediately hung up: twice she had admonished herself for her weakness.

Just before eleven, Katie began to sense the enveloping sadness that had previously heralded the appearance of the spectre. This time, however, the feeling disappeared as quickly as it began and, moments later, her Steve came through the door. Friday night at the club was his single vice, inherited from his father, but even so he stuck to a strict budget and always returned home when it was spent. Katie looked up and him and smiled as he entered the living room; in return, he bent down and kissed her tenderly on the lips. Not so long previously, that would have been a prelude to sex, but, at more than seven months pregnant, Katie's bump was large enough to interfere with the act of making love and Steve realised that his wife felt awkward and uncomfortable with the idea at this stage in her pregnancy. Nobody would have described Steve as a "new man", but he loved his wife enough to suppress his own

41

urges in order to spare Katie's discomfort. For her part, Katie was not only grateful for his loving concern but equally aware that she would enjoy making it up to him as soon as she was able. Instead, they held hands as they looked in on their slumbering son then headed off to bed. Katie decided that she would just enjoy having Steve beside her and save her story for the morning.

***

Tina Simpson made her way unsteadily up the path to her front door, regretting the mix of vodka and high heels. She had spent the evening in the Puss in Boots with Karen, with whom she had gone to school and who had been bridesmaid at her wedding. Karen, also divorced, had left the pub with one of the pair of younger men that had been gratifyingly attentive all evening. Tina had considered spending the night with the other man, but had decided that the embarrassment of waking up with somebody barely older than her son vastly outweighed the ephemeral physical pleasure that would doubtless have awaited her in the boy's bed. Karen had no such scruples; indeed, Tina had had a year or so of sexual profligacy following her fortieth birthday which had been ended by her contracting a sexually transmitted infection. The shame of being treated for gonorrhoea at the local hospital had made her feel, despite the professional assurances and non-judgemental kindness of the staff, cheap and contaminated.

Pausing at the front door to remove her shoes, she plucked the key from her handbag and quietly let herself into the house. Closing the door silently behind her, she tip-toed up the stairs, hoping to sneak past Michael's bedroom door.

"Mum, I need to talk to you". His voice made her jump.

"Can't it wait? I'm tired" said his mother.

"No. I need to speak to you now." There was a determination in his voice that Tina hadn't heard before and that slightly worried her.

"Okay. At least let me get changed first." Tina knew that she had to transform herself from 'Mrs Robinson' back in to plain 'Mum' before having a conversation with her son.

"Yeah, all right. I'll be in my room" he replied, still sounding somewhat different. Tina wondered whether he was going to complain about her nights out, but decided to let him speak first rather than pre-empt what might turn out to be something entirely different.

Tina couldn't help thinking that she might have been better off surrendering to the temptation of a lithe young body rather than the prospect of her son's angst. The thought was reinforced as she slipped off her dress, catching sight of herself in the mirror. I'm not bad for my age, she thought, wondering why she had bothered with a push-up bra and seamed stockings if she had no intention of using her feminine wiles for transient gratification. Dismissing the thought, she changed in to her least sexy pyjamas, removed her makeup and steeled herself for what Michael had to say.

"Mum, has anybody in our family ever been murdered?" His words left her speechless. Whatever she may have expected from him, this enquiry was straight from left field.

"Er...not that I can think of, love. Why do you ask?"

"It's...difficult to explain." Mike had no idea how to broach the subject of ghosts with his mother, although now that she looked like Mum rather than some desperate old tart he found speaking to her much easier. "I just had...a nightmare. I dreamt that somebody in our family had been killed in the past. It seemed so real, I thought that, well, maybe it may have been true."

Tina pondered for a moment. "The only person that I can think of would be my Grandad, but he wasn't murdered as such."

"What do you mean, 'as such'?" queried Mike, fixing his mother with an earnest look that un-nerved her all the more.

"Well, he was killed in the war. He was..." Mike interrupted her.

"A sailor?"

"Yes...in the merchant navy. As far as I know, his ship was torpedoed and there were no survivors. What made you say that?"

Mike smiled at her, the look in his eyes diminishing. "It was all in the dream, that's all. Thanks."

Saturday

George Williams' Saturday morning consisted of his weekly visit to Morrison's supermarket on Preston Docks. Just another anonymous pensioner among the throng, he stocked up on economy foods despite his railway pension giving him a reasonable income. Paying in cash as always, he loaded his shopping into a wheeled basket and headed for the bus stop. Outside, a cold breeze made him button his old woollen coat despite the spring sunshine. He resented what had become of the docks, once a thriving port reduced to an algae-ridden soup disturbed only by the ubiquitous gulls and the occasional yacht from the marina that had replaced the ocean-going cargo ships. On his side of the dock basin were "retail outlets", the chain stores offering consumer durables on cheap credit. Opposite were overpriced flats and houses, too expensive for the working class men that had toiled here for generations.

As he climbed onto the bus, the whistle of a steam train pierced the traffic noise. On the other side of the dock, the local heritage railway were running their former shunting engine along the line that passed alongside the dock, then crossed the dock entrance on a swing bridge leading to the museum building erected only a year or two previously. The shriek of the engine's whistle brought back quite different memories; of excitement, of fear, of shame. He had lived with his secret for so many years now, yet it still took him unawares whenever it surfaced. A few years previously, an article in the local newspaper had convinced him that his skeleton in the cupboard would be discovered and that he was to be exposed to ridicule and humiliation. After a nervous few days, he had realised that his guilt would remain undisturbed. He was the only one left now, the others were gone, one the victim of a Nazi shell in the Bocage and the other consumed by cancer ten years previously.

As always, when his memories intruded into the present, he reminded himself of the righteousness of his long-held cause. As always, it didn't quite work, the residual emotion being deepened as the bus dropped him off on Broadgate, next to Penwortham bridge. He had to walk the last couple of hundred yards home, passing the remains of the other, parallel bridge that had carried the West Lancashire railway across the Ribble. Only the stone supports remained, the metal lattice bridge having been demolished shortly after the line had closed more than forty years before. The old bridge had also carried a huge water pipe: this was still in place, incongruously clinging to one edge of the otherwise redundant stanchions. It was enough, however, to remind George of his culpability.

Looking between the budding boughs across the river, where the embankment on the Penwortham side ended, he thought he saw a movement in the trees.

"Kids" he muttered to himself. But something, just a feeling, made him look back.

***

Despite the threat of showers, Jack Rimmer had decided to spend Saturday afternoon tackling the jungle that sprawled outside his back door. He had been hard at it for over an hour, with little apparent progress. The previous day had been largely consumed by a search for Cedric Morgan's contact details which he had finally discovered in a totally unrelated folder full of newspaper cuttings and scribbled notes in the bottom drawer of the filing cabinet in his study. For a military man, Jack was surprisingly untidy. Although he had joined the army as a private, his natural leadership, coupled with his skill as a member of the Intelligence Corps, had led to his being selected for the Royal Military Academy at Sandhurst in the mid 1970's and his subsequent promotion to Lieutenant. Since then, he had lived in various officers' messes where the daily domestic chores had been undertaken by others for him. Over the fifteen years that he spent as an officer he had developed a rather laid-back attitude to household tasks and the fifteen years since he had left the army had seen little improvement. His efforts had borne fruit, however. He had an invitation to lunch with Morgan at his home the following day.

He was scraping debris from his elderly Flymo when he realised that the phone was ringing. Dropping the lawnmower, Jack made his way to the kitchen, certain that whoever it was would ring off just as he lifted the handset. He was almost disappointed when he heard a woman's voice rather than the hum of a disconnected line.

"Hello, is that Mr Rimmer?" The voice was familiar, but held a tremor of nervousness. "It's Katie Melling here, we met on Tuesday."

"Mrs Melling, of course, how nice to hear from you. What can I do for you?"

Her reply took him completely by surprise. "I'm not sure how to put this, but was your mother's name Dorothy?"

"Yes, it was. How did you know?" replied Jack, instantly curious. The response shook him to the core.

"Because..." she paused for a moment. " Mr Rimmer, it's because I think that your father is haunting our flat."

***

Katie spent the next fifteen minutes recounting the events of the past few days, occasionally glancing toward Joshua's room where her son was having his usual afternoon nap. The rapt silence at the other end made her increasingly nervous as she related what the apparition had looked like and how it had spoken to her. As she ended her tale, the silence continued.

"Mr Rimmer, please, *please* believe me. I'm not making it up." She was close to tears, and had twisted the phone cord tightly around her hand. It had taken her the whole morning to pluck up the courage to ring in the first place, and now it seemed that the one person that could provide her with answers thought that she had taken leave of her senses.

When Jack Rimmer spoke, his voice was guarded and distant. "Mrs Melling, I don't know what to say." Katie's heart sank and a tear trickled down her cheek. "I have never experienced anything like this before, and clearly I have no idea whether this is a figment of your imagination, a fanciful story dreamed up for some reason that I cannot fathom, or whether you are indeed telling the truth. My mother's name is a matter of public record, and I told you that my father had died before I was born. Even your description of this ghost could have come from the photo that I showed you."

The line was quiet again. Katie felt crushed, humiliated. She began to sob.

"Mrs Melling, Katie, please listen to me." Jack's voice was warmer, more conciliatory. "All this is obviously very real to you, so would you please give me a day or so to think about this? Give me your number, and I will speak to you on Monday, if that is convenient."

Katie wiped a tear from her eye. "Yes, Mr Rimmer. Monday will be fine. I'll be working in the afternoon, though." She gave him the number.

"Monday morning it is, then. Please don't be upset; try putting yourself in my position. This has all been rather sudden. Bye for now."

Katie put the phone down. He was right, of course. A story like that out of the blue: who would believe it? Before Katie could lapse into self-pity, she was brought back to reality by the simultaneous wriggling of her unborn child and a cry for attention from Joshua.

Steve had left early that morning, and because of that was still oblivious to Katie's experiences of the previous afternoon. As they stood in the kitchen washing up after tea, Katie filled him in on what had occurred over the past twenty-four hours or so.

"Do you think that he believed you?" Steve wondered how Katie's story would have come across to a total stranger over the phone.

"I don't know, Steve. He said that he would call back on Monday morning, so I suppose that I'll find out then." She thought for a moment. "Steve, can you get the morning off? I want you to be here if he calls."

Steve went through to the living room and made a brief call. Moments later, he returned.

"I've sorted it, love. I just have to do a bit tomorrow instead."

***

Mike had spent the day trying to stay out of trouble at work. His normal daydreaming, the source of most of his employer's complaints, was gone, substituted by a sudden and unfamiliar thirst for knowledge. In between serving early-season tourists with coffee he had busied himself with energetically cleaning tables; this activity required no thought whatsoever and what looked like conscientious application to a mundane task was actually an excuse to ruminate.

"Mike, a word please." Mike's heart sank as his manager called him over. Expecting the worst, Mike was about to tell the manager, who was all of twenty-six, where he could stick his job.

"Nice work today, Mike. Keep it up." Beaming his customary less-than-sincere smile, the manager turned and went back into the broom cupboard that passed for an office. So that's the secret, thought Mike. Just look busy, and the tinpot dictator will be fooled. He allowed himself a smile before finishing his current table and returning to his cogitation. Fortunately the spring sunshine was attracting customers to the coffee shop's pavement tables, so Mike increased the distance between himself and the manager by turning his attention to the outside.

He suspected that he had been visited by the ghost of his great-grandfather, who had obviously met a watery grave. There was no other explanation; not that any rational person would ever believe him. Mike knew that he needed to research that avenue further, but he was flummoxed by the rest of what he had been told. 'The signalman' suggested a railway, didn't it? As for the 'Penwortham Triangle', well, he had never heard of a place by that name, let alone a triangle associated with it. Would it be like the Bermuda Triangle, perhaps? The other question was: why now? What had happened to trigger these weird experiences? Mike had heard stories from his friends about hallucinations, but they had largely been induced by various illegal substances. Mike had only ever tried cannabis once: the experience had been one big anti-climax and the sudden disappearance of one of his college friends had led to speculation among his peers that the unfortunate boy had been committed to a psychiatric hospital suffering from acute paranoid schizophrenia. When that particular rumour was confirmed as being true, Mike had decided there and then never to touch anything like that. His peers, many of them regular users, had mocked him mercilessly to begin with, then simply ignored him. Mike was happy enough with that outcome: he found their obsession with sex and drugs deeply discomfiting and largely preferred his own company, or at least the company of his online opponents.

That evening Mike once again retreated into his bedroom, intent on a serious session with Google. Starting with information on the Merchant Navy, it became obvious quite quickly that, unless a family member had more information, the main source for research was the National Archive in London. A trip of that nature would be quite beyond Mike, who had never ventured further than Leeds on his own.

Further investigation failed to turn up a Penwortham Triangle, but did, at least, pinpoint the location of the town itself. The same web page had a map of the railways around Preston, which showed a Penwortham Junction. Also mentioned was a station, called Penwortham Cop Lane. What did stand out from the map was the layout of the railway: in several places three lines came together to form a triangle. This was good news.

The repository of much railway knowledge was on Mike's doorstep, at the National Railway Museum.

Sunday

The following day, as Steve Melling was closing the flat door behind him, Jack Rimmer was pacing the length of his study deep in thought. He simply could not believe the story that he had heard, yet he was struggling to come up with an explanation for why Katie had made the call in the first place. On balance, he decided, it was not an over-active imagination. There was too much detail in the story, and it would have taken more than a couple of days to determine his mother's name via the usual route. That left a deliberate hoax. But why? What did the Mellings hope to gain from such a story? Their meeting had been entirely coincidental and Jack was hardly the famous author of a series of blockbusters and so was a poor candidate for blackmail. And yet...the only remaining possibility was so improbable that even Sherlock Holmes would never have believed it. And yet... could it be the truth?

Jack had spent the majority of his working life gathering intelligence. Whilst his gut instinct told him that ghosts simply don't exist, the facts suggested that Katie Melling was telling him the truth. Looking at his watch, Jack made for his front door, grabbing his jacket and keys as he went.

Cedric Morgan lived some ninety minutes' drive from Jack's house in the village of Fletching in East Sussex. The village is what estate agents would describe as a "rural idyll", with short rows of tiny cottages, most with immaculate gardens, clustered around a medieval church and the ubiquitous public house.

Jack parked his car outside Cedric Morgan's white-fronted cottage just as the man himself was walking slowly toward him from the direction of the church. Now aged ninety-two, he leaned heavily on a walking stick and was accompanied by a tall, willowy woman of about Jack's age who fussed over him as he stumbled slightly whilst traversing a pothole.

"Ah, young Rimmer!" Jack smiled as Cedric lifted his cane in greeting. "Oh, do stop grabbing me, Janice," he said as the woman took his arm to stop him toppling over. "I'm not a total cripple, you know."

The woman looked at Jack and rolled her eyes. She was clearly used to Cedric's idiosyncrasies and ignored his grumpy entreaties whilst addressing Jack.

"You must be our last-minute lunch guest. I'm Janice Forsyth, your last-minute lunch cook. I'm also, for my sins, his daughter."

"Jack Rimmer. Please to meet you."

"Come on, you two," said Cedric, irritably. "Let's get inside. I'm hungry for food and a decent chin-wag."

Inside, the cottage was tiny. The front door opened straight into the living room which was dominated by a huge inglenook fireplace that took up most of the wall opposite the door. To the left of the fireplace was another door which led to three steps down to the kitchen and dining area. The small, round table was set for three and the smell of roasting beef filled the room.

"Sherry, Rimmer?" Cedric was definitely one of the old school for whom the use of surnames came close to an expression of friendship. Jack declined, pleading the necessity to drive home after their conversation. His reply was greeted with an almost derisive snort.

"So, what do you want to know?" the old man had a glint in his eye as he sat in an armchair with a schooner of Amontillado. "Looking to dig the dirt on some poor soul, are you?"

"Er...no. I just wanted to speak to you about a wartime case."

"Pity. Never mind. Which case are you interested in this time?"

"Sciron." Jack explained the background to his enquiry, leaving out the previous day's developments.

Cedric thought for a moment, running his gnarled hand through the shock of white hair that had clearly defied any attempt at grooming. "Ah, yes, the robber of antiquity. A very slippery character, as I recall. Led us quite a merry dance, that one. Do you know, we were convinced that he was a Soviet agent, but he turned out to be something quite different. One of Canaris' finest, I suspect, and probably the only one that had us fooled in the early years. Yes, very clever, our Sciron."

He paused, deep in thought. His eyes took on a faraway look and he appeared to be staring into space. "From what you tell me, he was probably responsible for the disappearance, or possibly the death of your father."

***

Mike Simpson had emerged from his room at the early, for him, time of eleven thirty. His shift pattern meant that, having worked Saturday, he had Sunday off. As Jack Rimmer and Cedric Morgan were conversing, Mike was cursing his inability to drive along with the infrequent Sunday bus service. He had walked most of the way into town before a bus came, catching him between two stops and unable to flag it down. Having reached the iron girder bridge that crossed the railway, he decided that he would save his money and walk the last mile and a half to the railway museum.

Finally reaching his destination, Mike wandered into the museum's City entrance. Unsure of what to say, and to whom, he nervously loitered in the entrance area, scanning the information on the walls around him. After a few minutes, a woman in the nearby gift shop caught his eye. Explaining that he was looking for information about the West Lancashire Railway, she directed Mike to the information point a few yards into the building. Thanking her, Mike made his way further into the museum. On duty at the information desk was a particularly attractive girl of about Mike's age: immediately his nerves worsened and his mission was temporarily forgotten as he wondered whether she would notice that he hadn't had a shower that morning. To make matters worse, the label with her name on was pinned perilously close to an eye-catching cleavage.

"Can I help?" Mike realised that the girl was looking straight at him.

"N..no. I mean..er..yes. I'm, er, looking for some information about a railway."

"Well, I'd say that you've come to the right place, then." Mike cringed inwardly as the girl fixed him with a thousand-watt smile. He couldn't place her accent: it sounded a bit like Geordie, but not as broad. Wherever it came from, it sounded like she was gently mocking him.

"No, I mean, a particular railway." Another horrific thought entered Mike's mind: would she think that he was a train spotter? Mike knew that he wasn't the coolest or most attractive man, but there were limits.

"Not that I'm a train spotter or anything," he added unnecessarily.

"It's okay," she said in a conspiratorial whisper. "Your secret's safe with me. Which railway were you looking for?"

Mike couldn't help noticing that her eyes were a deep shade of blue. "Er...the West Lancashire Railway. It's not there any more, but, I, er...need to find out about it for, er, my college course."

His relief at coming up with a reasonable explanation for his presence in the museum was short lived.

"Oh yes, what are you studying, then? I'm at the university too." Mike froze. He was utterly hopeless at this sort of off the cuff dissimulation. After what seemed like an eternity, he finally managed to reply.

"I'm not at the uni...I'm, er, at York College. Studying, er, history." He hoped that he had done enough to dig himself out of the hole that, as it happened, existed only in his own mind.

The girl looked at him for a second, then consulted the book in front of her.

"One moment," she said, picking up the phone on her desk. After a brief conversation, she once again made Mike feel uncomfortable as she looked him in the eye.

"The man that you need to speak to, apparently, isn't here today. He'll be in tomorrow, and each day next week, until we close at six." She handed Mike a slip of paper with the name of the man that she was referring to.

"Thanks, er, Emily" said Mike, using the name tag as an excuse to chance one more glance at her décolletage.

"You're welcome. Any time." The knowing tone in her voice was enough to send Mike scuttling away, berating himself for his incapability when it came to dealing with women. To add to his frustration, the bus timetable was working against him again, and he was forced to walk home, too.

Monday Morning

Steve and Katie had been looking forward to enjoying the luxury of a lie-in that Monday morning. Joshua, however, had other ideas; waking just after six as intent on play as only a toddler can be at that hour. Steve took him into the living room to give his wife another hour or so in bed, but their other child, obviously a quick learner, decided to join in the early morning fun.

Two hours later, the three of them were gathered in the living room, the adults still nursing coffee cups and Joshua engaged in the alternate construction and demolition of a Duplo tower. Just as Katie began to feel a now-familiar despondency, her son looked up from the multi-coloured mayhem surrounding him.

"Man coming" he said, pulling himself to his feet and toddling over to the window. Steve and Katie exchanged nervous glances.

"Do you feel it, Steve? The sadness? He's coming back."

The feeling of wretchedness intensified, making Katie shrink into her seat. Joshua was pointing out of the window, shouting.

"Look, Mummy, Daddy: Man!" Steve went over to the window and looked out, but, despite the uneasy feeling that was penetrating his consciousness, saw nothing. His wife's voice made him spin round.

"He's here."

Steve was rooted to the spot. The apparition that had haunted their lives for the past week was stood in the doorway to the living room, his coal-black eyes seemingly burning into Steve's mind.

Help me.

Steve realised that he had heard the words, but the spectre's lips hadn't moved. He tried to move to protect Katie, but found that his legs had turned to rubber and he found himself gripping the window ledge to prevent himself from falling over.

What happened to me? Where's Dot?

"She's not here. We don't know where she is." Katie's voice held none of the fear that paralysed Steve. "We don't know what happened to you, but we are trying to find out."

The figure in the doorway looked blankly at Steve for what seemed like an eternity. His gaze slowly shifted to Katie, and finally to Joshua. His grey, downturned mouth lifted slightly as he looked at the little boy, his expression almost resembling a smile. He looked up sharply, his demeanour returning to utter misery.

Why did he hit me?

Steve realised for the first time that the man in front of him had bloodstains down the side of his head, but, to his relief, his son was oblivious to the fact. He was amazed by Katie's seeming lack of fear as she addressed the nightmare vision that had invaded their home.

"Who hit you Jack?"

Can't...remember. Dark...so dark. I'm cold, Dot, and can't find my way home.

The ringing of the phone made Steve look away for a moment. When he looked back, the phantom had vanished.

"Man gone" burbled Joshua, knocking over another tower.

***

It had been a sleepless night for Jack Rimmer. Cedric Morgan's revelations about Sciron had reinforced Jack's growing suspicion that, despite its seeming implausibility, Katie Melling's story might just be genuine. Lunch had been a slightly strained affair, with Jack being careful not to blurt out any of the supernatural aspects that were foremost in his mind. Janice was clearly an excellent cook and her witty interjections had been something of a relief from her father's patrician lecturing. There were, however, some pieces of the puzzle missing, and Jack knew that his return to Lancashire could not be put off any longer.

His first task was to speak with Katie, as he had promised on the previous Saturday. He sat in his study, staring at the flock wallpaper that had been left behind by the last occupant of the house, going over in his mind the words that he would use. Finally, putting aside the irrelevant thought that he really must get around to redecorating, he could delay no longer. Locating the scrap of paper on which he had scribbled the Mellings' number, he lifted the handset and jabbed at the buttons.

"Mrs Melling, I think that I believe you" said Jack when Katie answered the phone. "I also think that I may know what happened to my father, although I need to find out a few things first."

"You should have phoned a few minutes earlier," Katie's voice still had a slight tremor that unnerved Jack. "Your father was just here, and this time Steve saw him."

Jack was utterly lost for words. The ensuing heavy silence was punctuated only by the unfettered chattering of the toddler at the other end. When Jack finally regained his composure, it was all he could do to tell Katie that he would be making his way back up north, and to ask when it would be convenient for him to call in.

Jack went over in his mind his itinerary for his forthcoming trip. He would have to visit the local newspaper archives, and further research what his father may have been doing to bring about his disappearance. He now knew, from the archive and Morgan's recollections, of the events of April 1941 and the part played by the foreign spy. What he could not know was whether his father had been an active participant, a witness, an innocent victim or if his disappearance the same night was some sort of bizarre coincidence.

Having booked a room at the same motel that he had stayed in the previous week, Jack went to his bedroom to pack his bag. He planned to do no more than to travel north that day, access the newspaper archives the following day then visit the Mellings on Wednesday morning before returning home. Counting out the requisite clean clothing, he carefully placed it in the green nylon holdall that had served him for the previous ten years or so, and then moved to the bathroom for his toiletries. Once there, he caught sight of himself in the mirror: the dark rings under his eyes accentuating his lined face. Suddenly he felt very, very lonely. He had chatted with Janice the previous afternoon whilst Cedric had taken a post-prandial nap, and had been impressed with her *joie de vivre*. She, too, lived alone, but in her case because she had been widowed some seven years previously. Unlike Jack, she had the comfort of three children and no fewer than eight grandchildren to alleviate her solitude.

Jack's life had always revolved around the Army. On the few occasions that he had fallen in love, the object of his desire had been wholly unsuited to military life and none had persuaded him to give up his vocation. Most of the time, Jack was quite happy with his bachelorhood but occasionally, like today, the realisation that he was likely to end his days alone forced its way to the front of his consciousness. It took a considerable effort of will to continue his packing but he was still distracted by the emotion as he loaded his bag into his car. As he reversed off the drive, alternate feelings of loneliness interspersed with uninvited thoughts of Janice's sparkling blue eyes diverted his attention, just for a moment.

That moment was enough. The impact threw his head against the side window just as he became aware of the shrieking of rubber against tarmac. Jack was dazed, unable to move. Without really thinking about it, he managed to switch off the engine and remove his seat belt. He tried to open the door, without realising that a blue Renault Clio was jammed into the side of his car. Jack became dimly aware that somebody was talking to him and at that moment his head began to hurt. The pain was intense, like a hammering inside his skull. It brought him round, however, and he turned to the person that had opened the passenger door.

"Are you all right? What happened?" The voice of his neighbour finally penetrated the mist in Jack's head.

"I've no idea. One moment I'm reversing off the drive, then...this."

"Are you hurt? Should I call an ambulance?" The concern in the man's voice suggested to Jack that he ought to check whether he had indeed been injured. Holding his hand against the side of his head that had impacted the window, he was mildly surprised to see that he was not bleeding.

"It's just a bang on the head, I think. I'll be fine. What about the other driver?"

The neighbour, whose name Jack couldn't remember, went around the front of the car to the smaller car embedded in it. As he did so, Jack heaved himself across the passenger seat and half fell out of the car. As he regained his feet, he saw the other driver, a youth of about twenty, leaning on his wrecked pride and joy. On seeing Jack he started towards him.

"You stupid old git! Look what you've done to my motor!"

As he spoke, the wail of sirens could be heard from behind Jack, causing the young man to stop in his tracks. Hurling a few choice expletives, he ran away from the approaching police car.

Jack felt utterly confused, like a first-time spectator at a baseball game, as the police car pulled up. He was still staring, open-mouthed, as one of the uniformed occupants came over to him.

"Do you need medical attention, Sir?" said the policeman.

"I don't think so," said Jack, curious as to what had transpired with the other driver. "The other driver...why did he run away?"

"Can't say, but I've no doubt that we'll find no record of any insurance. Speaking of which, since you appear to be unhurt, would you mind producing your documents, Sir?"

Forty minutes later, having pushed the badly-damaged Honda on to the drive and satisfied the local constabulary with his licence, insurance and MOT certificate, Jack unpacked his laptop. While it was booting up, he called his insurers to report the accident and arrange for the car to be inspected.

Having arranged with them to collect the keys from the neighbour and checked the train times from Ashford station via the national rail website, Jack rang a taxi and repacked his computer. Making his way outside with his bags, he leaned on the boot of his wrecked car.

"Are you all right, Mr Rimmer?" The voice belonged to his other neighbour, a slightly-built divorcee of approximately fifty who nurtured an unrequited desire that Jack would one day notice her. "I hope you didn't mind me calling the police, only..."

"Thank you, no, I don't mind at all. I rather think that you may have saved me from an even more unpleasant experience." Jack had, in fact, noticed her and found her quite attractive. The attraction, however, was not enough for him to overcome his reluctance to begin a relationship. What if it didn't work out? She would still be his neighbour and...it was all too risky for Jack.

As she opened her mouth to speak again, a silver Nissan saloon pulled up outside Jack's house. Salvation, thought Jack, speaking before she could prolong the exchange.

"That'll be my taxi. Thanks again." Jack smiled graciously at her, threw his bags on the back seat then sat next to the driver, glad that the car's arrival had also saved him from a slightly awkward conversation.

***

Public transport was a revelation to Jack Rimmer. He had travelled on rail warrants during his military career; the intervening years had dulled his memory of the experience. Arriving at Ashford station, he purchased a return ticket to Preston. That was the first shock: having to part with over £250 unless he could commit to a particular train for his return journey. Arriving on the platform as a London train pulled in, it took Jack a moment or two to realise that the doors opened at the push of a button. Sitting on a narrow, gaudily upholstered seat with cigarette burns in the fabric and discarded chewing gum on the floor, he placed his suitcase and laptop bag on the seat next to him.

Not realising that he had caught a stopping train, Jack became increasingly frustrated as the train halted every few minutes. Each halt was accompanied by a computer generated voice informing him of the stops to come, the next stop, the train company's smoking policy and advising him to keep his luggage with him at all times. By the fourth stop, Hollingbourne, he was losing the will to live. He knew that the distance from Ashford to London was about fifty-five miles, and alleviated the sheer boredom of the journey by calculating that his average speed was about thirty-seven miles per hour. Well, at least it was faster than the M25. Just.

The open country of Kent finally gave way to the suburban sprawl that is London, and eventually, nearly ninety minutes after leaving his adopted home town, Jack was crossing the Thames into London's Victoria station. Retrieving his suitcase, Jack cursed silently as he stepped in the sticky, glutinous mass that he had assiduously avoided for the past hour and a half. Unsuccessfully attempting to scrape the sole of his shoe clean, he resigned himself to sticking to the floor with every step. Still muttering to himself, he alighted from the train and made his way to the Underground.

Here little seemed to have changed, visually at least. The station was as he remembered them, the map as confusing as ever. Having deciphered the multi-coloured ribbons, Jack was delighted to discover that a direct train would get him to his next destination, Euston, in under ten minutes.

Jack struggled with his bags down the escalators to the Victoria Line platform. Here another surprise awaited him. Despite being the middle of the day, the platform was heaving with people. Fighting his way down the platform, Jack was astounded to hear people conversing in a plethora of different languages, many of which he recognised as eastern European. English speakers appeared to be in the minority, and Jack wondered how things could have changed so much since the last time that he had used this means of crossing the capital.

A train arrived, and the mass of humanity surged forward as the doors opened, heedless of the people trying to get off. Being laden with bags, Jack had great difficulty in battling his way on to the train, finally cramming himself into a tiny space against the glass partition close to the door. He was amazed that so many bodies could fit into such a small space; a glance around the carriage at the faces of his fellow travellers told him that either everybody accepted the crush with great stoicism, or that this situation was entirely normal. Fortunately, it was only four stops to Euston, but, even so, the temperature in the carriage quickly became most uncomfortable and Jack felt himself begin to perspire.

His ordeal was soon over. After just eight minutes feeling sympathy for sardines, Jack was able to leave the train and be swept along with the multitude to the main line station.

***

"Have you two had a fight?"

Katie's mother wasn't the best judge of mood or character, but even she had noticed the atmosphere in the Mellings' flat when she had arrived for her usual childcare stint.

"No, Mum, everything's fine." Katie's demeanour was fairly normal; it was Steve who had not seemed his usual self. He had left for work almost without a word, not even one of his habitual mother-in-law jibes.

Katie readied herself for a shift at the Spar shop, and could hear Joshua becoming fractious in the living room as she struggled to pull on her knee-length boots.

"He was up early this morning, Mum," she explained. "He'll be ready for his nap". With that she put on her coat, gave her son and mother each a quick peck on the cheek and headed out of the flat.

At the bottom of the stairs she was surprised to see her husband waiting for her.

"I'll walk you to work," he said, taking her arm. "What are we going to do, love? What's happening to us? I've never felt so frightened as this morning, and I think that it's more because I couldn't do anything. I was useless, wasn't I?"

"At least you stayed conscious," Katie replied. I fainted the first time I saw him, remember?"

"'Him'? Don't you mean 'it'?"

"He was a man once. Besides, you've heard him: he's confused, lost. He can't remember what happened to him. He's probably been floating around here for years, and it wasn't until the flats were built that he could actually speak to anybody."

"You're talking like you know what's going on here!" Steve's voice had an edge of exasperation. Katie's attitude towards this upheaval in their lives was turning their normal relationship on its head: *he* was supposed to be the sensible one, the decisive one, the calm one in a crisis. Indeed, he had played that role ever since they had met six years previously. It was he who had approached Katie in the Labour club, where she was working her first night behind the bar, and asked her on a date. It was he who had gone out and spent the traditional month's wages on an engagement ring when Katie had tremulously informed him that she was pregnant with Joshua, then overcome the objections of Katie's mother to their marriage. It was he who had remained calm when she had gone into labour three weeks early in the early hours of the morning.

So why was he going to pieces now? How could she be so accepting of this impossible situation? Steve shook his head and pulled his wife closer to him as they walked.

"Okay, love," he said. "It's 'him'. So what do we do about him?"

"We find out what happened to him."

***

The journey appeared to be improving. The Pendolino train looked sleek and modern in the platform at Euston station, its appearance marred only by the multitude of dead insects splattered across the otherwise bright yellow cab. Jack walked along the platform looking for the standard class carriages, deciding to head for the front of the train. On reaching it, he was delighted to see that the very front coach was designated a "quiet zone", with the use of mobile phones prohibited. Heaving his bags through the door, the sleek exterior gave way to a somewhat cramped interior. There was a single small luggage rack, which was already full despite there being only half a dozen people in the carriage. Finding an unreserved seat, Jack crammed his laptop bag and suitcase into the overhead rack and sat next to the narrow window.

Within a few minutes, the carriage was almost full. Jack's heart sank as the prospect of a quiet journey receded with the arrival of a gargantuan couple with a gaggle of noisy children. The woman, her unwashed hair scraped back into a flaccid ponytail, was bellowing obscenities into her phone whilst simultaneously berating one of her brood for some minor misdemeanour. Clearly oblivious to the spirit of the quiet zone, the male was generously sharing the contents of his personal stereo with everybody. Jack couldn't help wondering whether the man was stone deaf, given the volume at which the "music" was playing.

Since this large, in both senses of the word, family hadn't reserved any seats, they found themselves scattered around the carriage. To Jack's horror, the woman spotted the empty seat next to him and, without a word, sat in it. The stench of body odour made Jack gag, but he was stuck. His natural reticence, the curse of the English gentleman, would not allow him to get up and move seats, not that there were any more seats to be had. His nerves were frayed by the woman's phone ringing again, the loud jarring ringtone obviously designed to cause as much offence as possible.

When the woman's conversation informed him that the family were bound for Blackpool, and would therefore be on the train until Preston, Jack resigned himself to his fate. Fine Army officer you are, he thought to himself. But at the same time he recognised that his unwelcome neighbour was unlikely to respond to reasoned requests for peace and quiet, a view reinforced by her foul-mouthed tirade at a bespectacled six-year-old who was happily creating body art on his younger sister with a biro.

A few minutes later (although it seemed far longer to Jack) the train began to move out of the station. The woman celebrated this fact by opening a large packet of crisps and beginning to stuff them unceremoniously into her mouth. The smell of cheese and onion partially masked her natural scent, but that was of little consolation to Jack. As the train gathered speed, an announcement by the "train manager to all customers" informed him that the first stop for the train would be Milton Keynes, in approximately half an hour. Jack determined at that point to leave the train there and catch the next one, however long he may have to wait. Even an hour or so in Milton Keynes had to be preferable to two hours next to this ghastly woman. The decision made, Jack's mind moved on to wondering what had happened to "guards and passengers" on trains.

Thirty minutes later, Jack was standing on the platform at Milton Keynes Central station. The grey skies were emitting a fine drizzle that matched the soulless concrete of the station buildings and Jack's increasingly foul mood. He had extricated himself from his seat after politely informing his neighbour that this was his stop. Her reaction had been a look of exasperated indignation: rolling her eyes as if Jack had suggested relieving her of her second crisp packet. Jack's demeanour was not helped by the total absence of anybody on the platform to tell him when the next train to Preston might be. Making his way up the stairs to the main concourse, he was aghast to discover that the next direct train would be in two hours' time. He had the option of waiting half an hour and changing at Crewe, which at least got him to Preston only one hour later than the original train. By this time, Jack was thoroughly dejected and feeling just a little foolish. All because he had not been paying attention as he reversed out of his drive! This thought reminded him of the reason for his absent-mindedness, and mental images of Janice lightened his mood slightly. Old fool, he reflected, she'll not be interested in you. But he was still thinking about her as be boarded the somewhat less crowded Liverpool-bound train to continue his journey.

Monday Afternoon

The weather front that was the cause of the miserable conditions in Milton Keynes had yet to reach Preston, but to those that recognise the signs its approach was signalled by a thin layer of high cloud that had begun to mask the lowering sun. Kevin Anderson, not being one of those who could, simply muttered under his breath that it had turned cold again. He had just walked out of the Bridge Inn, the hostelry located adjacent to the eighteenth-century Penwortham Bridge that joined that town to Preston. Having run out of money, Kevin used the bridge to cross the river towards George Williams' house.

Kevin was a regular visitor to that house, in fact the only regular visitor, apart from the postman. The Victorian semi-detached house had seen better days, although Kevin did his best to help the old man out by doing odd jobs such as clearing out the gutters and exterior painting. Kevin knocked on the door that he had painted the previous summer and waited for George to answer.

"Afternoon, Grandad," said Kevin, brightly. George grunted an inaudible reply and motioned for him to come in. The hallway was windowless and dim; the house smelled of that peculiar odour that Kevin would always associate with his genuine grandparents.

"Kettle's on. Make us a brew." George was in one of his moods, thought Kevin. He had noticed that, despite being generally grumpy, George occasionally descended into a far blacker disposition. Today was one of those days, and Kevin was never sure whether to ask him about it or just ignore his demeanour. Today, however, Kevin had drunk just enough to suppress his inhibitions, and besides, he really did care about the old bloke in his own way.

"What's the matter, Grandad? Somebody died?" Kevin wasn't known for his tact, but George's reaction wiped the smile from his face.

"Yes," he hissed. "A very long time ago, but I keep getting the feeling he's come back."

* * *

On his arrival in Preston, Jack realised that he had another problem. He had booked a room in the Holiday Inn Express that he had stayed in on his previous visit, which was located just off the M6 some miles to the south of the centre of Preston. Additionally, he had arrived during rush hour and there were no taxis at the station's front entrance. Jack found himself wandering up the slope out of the station, unsure what to do next. Get a grip, he thought, chastising himself for his indecision. At the top of the incline, he looked around and saw that the city centre appeared to be to his right. Setting off in that direction, he realised that he had not eaten since breakfast and was suddenly very hungry. Fortunately it was only a few minutes before he came across a small cafe bar on the opposite side of the road and, making his way between the stationary vehicles waiting at the traffic lights, went inside.

Perusing the menu, he decided upon pasta carbonara and garlic bread washed down with a large glass of Chianti. As his meal was being prepared, Jack called over the waitress to ask if he could borrow their phone book. Finding the number of his hotel, he rang to see whether he could cancel his booking. Having been informed that he would have to pay for that night regardless, he decided that he would get a taxi out to the hotel after he had eaten and see about hiring a car in the morning.

His food arrived, and Jack wolfed it down hungrily. He was careful not to drink the wine that had preceded the meal, knowing that it would have gone straight to his head. The cafe bar was busy, but his table's location in the back corner ensured that he was not unduly disturbed by the to-ing and fro-ing of other customers. Having finished his meal, he asked the waitress to arrange for a taxi to take him out to his hotel, and ordered another glass of wine while he waited.

***

Kevin Anderson was confused. "What d'ya mean, he's come back? Like a ghost or summat?"

"No idea. It's just that...oh, I don't know. Maybe I'm going senile or something." There was a tiredness in George's voice that was so pronounced even Kevin noticed it. The old man was normally so fired up when he was lecturing to his cabal in the club that it came as a shock to the normally thoroughly insensitive younger man. Perplexed by what he had heard, Kevin scuttled into George's kitchen to make them both a brew. On his return, two steaming mugs grasped in his large hands, George was standing in his front room staring out of the window.

"Ever done something that you regret, Kevin? I mean, *really* regret?"

The old man's question did nothing to ease his visitor's bewilderment. Before he could string together a coherent response, George continued.

"Long time ago, I did something that I believed to be right. Direct action, they call it now. Trouble is, somebody got in the way. Wasn't my fault, he wasn't supposed to be there. Nobody was supposed to get hurt." The tiredness was gone now, replaced by barely suppressed anger.

The old man turned toward Kevin. "But I had to do it, didn't I? It was for the cause! Sixty-five years I've lived with it! So why now? Why is he coming back now?" There was an edge of hysteria in his voice now, his face was florid and his hands had begun to shake. Kevin was standing in front of him, mouth agape, his eyes flicking between George and the front window, as if there was an answer to his confusion outside. Eventually, the pain of the hot mugs fought its way through to his overloaded brain, forcing him to put them down on the occasional table next to the old man's armchair.

The movement seemed to diffuse the tension. George slumped into his armchair, his chin on his chest. After a moment, he lifted his eyes and looked at Kevin.

"Sit down, lad." Kevin duly obliged, taking a surreptitious peek out of the window as he did so.

"What did they teach you about the war at school? Do you think that we won it?"

"Well, er... o' course we did. Didn't we?"

"No, lad. The Great Patriotic War was won with the blood of millions of workers. Good Communists, every one of them. The Red Army won the war, lad, not the British, or the Americans, who both hid behind cowardly terror bombing." He paused for a moment, enjoying the rapt attention of his pupil. "But the Red Army didn't get involved until the Nazis turned on them. They had a pact, you see, an agreement that they wouldn't attack each other. Comrade Stalin was as good as his word, but the Nazis real target was the Soviet Union, and the destruction of international socialism."

George paused again as he could see the confusion in Kevin's face.

"Which war we talkin' 'bout? I thought that you was talkin' about world war two. What's this...what you called it?" Kevin's forehead was furrowed with concentration as he attempted to understand what the old man was saying.

"The Great Patriotic War, lad. That's what the Soviets called it. Anyway, at first, we in the Communist party decided that we would do nothing to help the war effort as long as Stalin and Hitler were allies. We just organised peace marches and made sure that the workers weren't being exploited any more than usual."

George stopped once more, sighing deeply and holding his head in his hands. Kevin slurped noisily at his tea, earning himself a withering look of reproach from his elder companion.

"Then, one day, a Comrade told us that the British government were going to supply arms to the Finns. These arms were going to support an invasion of the Soviet Union, sponsored by Churchill with his hatred for socialism. They had a ship disguised as a Swedish vessel, because the Swedes were neutral, which was coming into Preston docks for a cargo of ammunition. Well, we just had to stop it, don't you see? We *had* to!"

***

To Katie, the visitations were becoming familiar, almost routine. Steve still hadn't returned from work: the lengthening days meant that they could catch up on jobs that had been delayed or cancelled due to bad weather. Joshua was still up and about, running around the flat in his Thomas the Tank Engine pyjamas.

"Man coming, Mummy," he said just as Katie began to sense the sadness that accompanied the apparition whenever he put in an appearance. The sight of him still had the power to shock, however, and when the gaunt figure manifested in the hallway Katie's heart skipped a beat and her unborn child squirmed in response to the flow of adrenaline that resulted.

She's gone, isn't she? My Dorothy...where am I?

"Yes, I think that she is. It's been a long time, Jack. Your baby is an old man now. You've been gone a long time." Katie couldn't know for sure, but in her heart she believed that the ghost was, or had been, Jack Rimmer's father.

The baby...I have a son?

The haggard face was transformed at the news, eyebrows lifting, softening the expression from total misery to a hopeful pleading. Katie had a sudden feeling of self-doubt. What was she playing at? What would happen if she were wrong? She decided to change the subject.

"What happened to you, Jack? You said that somebody hit you. Who was it?" There was a pause, punctuated by Joshua's greeting of "Hello, man!" as he toddled from the living room to his bedroom for a different toy. The sadness returned to the phantom's face as his eyes seemed to bore into Katie's inner being.

It was... my friend? No...it can't have been...he's...somebody on the pole, cutting the wires...that's why the lamp's out...train... danger!

"What train? I don't understand! What do you mean, on the pole?" Katie could already feel his presence receding, as if the effort of manifestation had drained whatever energy he needed to appear. She realised that she had been given another piece of the puzzle, not that it made any sense to her. Fear had given way to frustration, firstly with the enigma of how the man died, but also an increasing feeling that she may never be rid of the spectre unless...what? That was another problem: how to lay the ghost to rest, to give him peace.

Casting these thoughts aside for the moment, Katie went to the kitchen. Having put the kettle on, she found the pad that she used for compiling shopping lists and wrote down everything that she could remember. Being bent over writing left her with backache, and she grimaced as she straightened herself, hands on her hips, with her fingers pressing into the small of her back. Hearing Steve come through the door, she took a second cup from the cupboard and listened with unalloyed pleasure as her husband greeted their son by lifting him above his head, making the boy shriek with delight.

A minute or so later, he came into the kitchen as Katie poured steaming water into the cups. Placing his arms tenderly around her waist, he nuzzled her neck before speaking.

"Perfect timing. I'm gasping! Got another garden finished off, so we can move on to that big landscaping job off Factory Lane tomorrow. There's good money in that one, should come in handy when number two puts in an appearance! Speaking of putting in appearances, has our friend Jack been back?"

"Which one? Living or dead?" Katie smiled grimly, continuing before her husband could react. "As a matter of fact, yes. The dead one, that is. He told me something about a pole, a lamp and a train."

"Eh? What...oh...I'm too tired for this. Our other friend is supposed to be coming tomorrow, isn't he? We'll have to figure it all out then."

***

That other friend was, at that moment, sat in his hotel room trying, unsuccessfully, to arrange a hire car for the following day. It had become clear by this point that he would be delayed in getting started the next morning while he rang round the local car hire depots. Instead, he turned his attention to the online archives of the local newspaper. These would clearly only cover a limited period, but Jack considered the effort worthwhile, if only to see if there was a particular event that may have triggered the Mellings' experiences.

Jack used various combinations of key words in the search facility but each was either too vague, throwing up hundreds of related articles, or so specific that the phrase "Your search generated no hits" began to grate on Jack's nerves. By eleven thirty, he was considering giving up for the night when his latest series of words, which were becoming increasingly convoluted and obscure, gave only eight potential articles. At last, thought Jack, something worth looking at.

Of course, it was the seventh article that finally showed some promise. The search criteria meant that the first six all contained stories describing personal tragedy, from the unmitigated devastation of a parent at the loss of a child to an unexplained suicide, each distilled into a microcosm of individual calamity rendered inconsequential by the hackneyed clichés of junior reporters. Jack knew from experience that the press, local or national, rarely reported either accurately or completely, and he supposed that what he was reading would be no different. That seventh piece seemed to be what he was looking for, although, rather than providing unambiguous answers, it posed a series of questions that Jack knew meant yet more research on his part.

Briefly scanning the final story, Jack confirmed its irrelevance to his quest before re-reading the article that had attracted his interest. Certain that he now had part of what he was looking for, he saved the story on to his laptop, then shut it down and retired for the night.

Tuesday Morning

Joshua was in tears. Katie had found him tearing pages from the phone book and putting them in his mouth: his lips and fingers were now grey and there were small fingerprints all over the living room wall. His face was at once both distraught and comical, and his mother was having difficulty keeping a straight face as she gently castigated him.

Their discussion was interrupted by the ringing of the door bell. Katie opened the door to find a haggard-looking Jack Rimmer waiting: she was immediately struck by the similarity between her current visitor and the spectral one.

"Mr Rimmer, please come in."

"Please, call me Jack. There's no need to stand on ceremony for me. Besides, I think that I may have some news for you."

Katie led him into the living room, where a subdued toddler was standing in the middle of the small space not occupied by furniture.

"I may have news for you too, Mr...Jack," said Katie. "I just need to clean up little Joshua first."

As Katie removed the print from her son with a baby wipe, Jack told her what he had discovered the previous night.

"I found the story on the website of the Lancashire Evening Post. Apparently, when the railway embankment was being cleared to make space for this estate, some human remains were found. The skeleton of a man, aged about forty, was unearthed by a mechanical digger. The skull had a large depression on one side, suggesting that the man had suffered a blow to the head."

"Was it the right side of his head?" asked Katie.

"Er, they didn't say." Jack was taken aback by the comment. "What makes you say that?"

"Our visitor has blood all down the right side of his face. And he says that somebody hit him. Last night he said 'he's my friend', but I don't know if he was talking about who hit him. He also said something about a pole and a lamp, but I've no idea what that means."

"Can you remember exactly what he said?" Jack's former life as an intelligence officer began to assert itself.

"Hang, on, I wrote it down," Katie went into the kitchen, returning a few moments later with a spiral-bound notepad. "He said... somebody up the pole, cutting wires, that's why the lamp's out. At least, I think that's it. It didn't make any sense."

"It makes sense to him. We'll just have to work out why it was important."

***

Jack Rimmer's condition had been caused by a sleepless night. He felt that he was so close now to discovering what had happened to his father, and it was that thought, endlessly churning about his mind, that had kept him awake until the early hours. Thoughts of where his father's remains may be, and how he ended up in his makeshift grave in the first place, had spun and swirled around his head, denying him the blessed release of slumber.

His alarm had erupted into his dreams at seven; his list of tasks for the day had not diminished just because of a bad night. After showering, shaving and dressing, Jack had eaten a leisurely breakfast in the pub adjacent to the motel before beginning his search for a hire car. A local company had a car ready for immediate hire and agreed to deliver it within the hour. His next port of call had been the Mellings' flat; following his conversation with Katie he drove into the city centre in search of the library.

The Harris building was, to Jack, a stunning example of Victorian philanthropy. Opened in 1893, it had been built with a legacy from a Preston lawyer. A colossus of neo-classical grandeur, its original exterior was marred by a covering of nets to keep the stone free from the detritus of the plethora of pigeons that inhabited the stone market square facing the front of the building; this consisted of a sculptured pediment atop an impressive colonnade. Unusually for a building in this style, there was no grand central staircase at the front, instead separate entrances at either side, modified to reflect modern sensitivities, allowed access to the atrium and thence the central hall. Jack, drawn to this huge chamber, found himself marvelling at its immense elegance, from the slightly uneven marble mosaic floor to the lantern tower which must have been, Jack thought, at least a hundred feet above his head. Taking the door straight ahead, he found himself in the lending library, where a young Muslim woman wearing a hijab directed him back to the entrance.

In the entrance hall, a pair of stone staircases led left and right to the first floor, the location of a museum and Jack's intended destination: the reference library. Taking the stairs to the right, he passed a Roll of Honour, the names of local men killed in the First World War. The sight of this reminded Jack about his long-dead uncle, probably commemorated in like manner a few miles away in his father's home town of Southport. The sombre, respectful carvings soon gave way to an exhibition by a local artist: Jack's first thought, that it must have been the work of nursery age children, soon gave way to the realisation that this was what is euphemistically termed "modern" art.

At the top of the first flight of stairs was a short landing and double doors leading to the museum and reference library. Spotting the latter to his right and passing through the open door, Jack found himself standing in front of an information desk. A somewhat overweight man, wearing a pale yellow shirt and an exasperated expression, was talking quietly on the telephone. Acknowledging his presence with a wave of his hand, he quickly concluded his conversation and turned his attention to Jack.

"Sorry about that. How can I help you?"

Jack explained what he had come for, and was led to a group of viewing machines; some with people sat at them, their faces illuminated by the screens; some with "Out of Order" notices on them, just to the left of the main desk. The librarian selected a roll of film from an adjacent drawer and fed it into one of the vacant machines.

Following a few brief instructions how to advance, rewind and rotate the images, Jack was left to his own devices. The first thing that he noticed was the name of the newspaper: in 1941 it was called the Lancashire Daily Post, and was priced at 1 ½ d. The sight of the old penny symbol unleashed a wave of nostalgia in Jack, not least memories of his mother giving him sixpence to go to the cinema on a Saturday morning, or the excitement generated by the sight of a ten shilling note in his birthday card.

The front page stories were all resolutely upbeat: how Luftwaffe raiders had been shot down or why the Axis forces could never win. Jack had to go deeper into the papers to find any hint that the British people were actually on the receiving end of any hostilities, and even then the articles were limited to vague allusions to bombing raids "somewhere in the North West". Finally, he found what he was looking for.

It was tucked away on page five, neatly sandwiched between a war-winning message to children from Togs the Terrier and a sublimely kitsch advertisement for "Mazo: the new wonder washing tablets". An announcement that train services to Southport would be disrupted for a few days "due to engineering work" had appended, almost as an afterthought, the news that a railway signalman was missing. That's it, thought Jack, another piece of the puzzle. Even as the notion crossed his mind he realised that some elements were still missing: the identity of his father's assailant being one.

Peter Thornhill was past seventy. He had joined British Railways in Crewe at the age of fifteen and had worked his way up from being a cleaner, through fireman to being a driver in the dying days of steam traction. After fifty years' service he had retired, moved to York, then gone back to work as a volunteer at the National Railway Museum. Having spent his career on the western side of the Pennines, he was the resident expert on the former London Midland region of the nationalised railway. In his seven years at the museum, he had shared his knowledge with many people, but few, if any, had looked quite like the young man who had presented himself at the information desk ten minutes earlier.

Mike Simpson had worked a double shift the previous day, another first for him. Today he was due to work the afternoon session beginning at two. He had amazed his mother by being out of bed at the unheard-of hour of eight that morning, actually eaten some breakfast then set off into the city centre and thence to the museum. He had half hoped that the information desk would be manned by the same girl as Sunday: when it turned out to be a man in his fifties he couldn't decide whether he was relieved or disappointed. Pushing these thoughts aside, he asked for the man whose name he had been given.

"What can I do for you, young man?" asked Peter, wondering why he had been asked for by name. Mike decided to stick with his earlier ruse.

"I'd like some information on the Penwortham Triangle, please. I'm...er...researching former Lancashire railways for my history project." Mike could feel his face redden as the lie passed his lips.

"Are you indeed?" Peter thought for a moment, then beckoned Mike to follow him. They walked for what seemed like an age, through the cavernous main hall that held the priceless collection of locomotives from a replica of the Rocket to a colossal steam engine that had seen service in China. Finally, they entered a side room and Peter took down a manila folder from a shelf. Humming to himself, he flicked through the pages, pausing briefly at one page before shaking his head and continuing. After another half minute, he stopped and put the folder down on the small table that nestled against the wall.

"Ah, yes. Here we are. Let me see...it was the West Lancashire railway which ran between Preston and Southport. Oh, it looks like it wasn't a true triangle at all for very long. See here." His finger pointed to a black and white map. "The three points of the triangle are all junctions. To the north, just on the riverbank, is Ribble Junction. That's the name of the river, you see. Directly south of that is Penwortham Junction, then to the east, you'll see that the tracks don't actually join up." The old man's speech was getting faster, his enthusiasm for his subject getting the better of him. "They would have joined at one point, but on this map...it's dated in the mid-thirties...that leg of the triangle is just a couple of long sidings."

Mike was thoroughly bemused by this point. The Thomas the Tank Engine phase of his life was many years in the past and hadn't lasted long anyway. But there was no holding back Peter, who was perusing another book.

"Yes, here it is. Middleforth Junction. The signal box was closed in 1905. Fascinating!" Mike realised that Peter was actually talking to himself, as if he had forgotten that he was not alone.

"Could I take a copy of that map?" asked Mike. Peter looked at him blankly for a moment. "What...hmm...yes, of course. A copy. Follow me!"

Twenty minutes later, Mike left the museum armed with an annotated copy of the eighty-year-old map. Walking towards the city centre and his place of employment, he realised that he had no idea what to do next.

Tuesday Afternoon

The past few days had been a revelation to Steve Melling. Features of the world around him had taken on a new significance. Some areas of his local environment were now explained; not that the lack of explanation had ever bothered him before. The strange wall outside his front window had become a bridge, carrying steam trains to Southport. To Steve, that particular seaside resort was accessible only by bus, which was why he hadn't been there since his childhood.

As he crossed Penwortham Bridge on his way home, he noticed for the first time the date carved into the stone wall: 1759. For a moment, Steve had a sense of history, of the innumerable pairs of feet that had preceded his own. He even found himself wondering, as he reached the Penwortham side of the river, just how old the pub associated with the bridge might be. Looking across the road at the primrose yellow building, he saw a familiar figure sat at one of the benches outside.

"Hiya, Kev," called Steve from the opposite side of the road.

Kevin Anderson, for once, did not have a pint of lager in front of him. Startled by Steve's greeting, he meekly raised one beefy hand in acknowledgement.

"What's up, no pint?" asked Steve, smiling. "That's not like you; are you ill or something?"

"Er...no. I'm fine. Not sure about old George, though. He keeps talking about some bloke that died years ago. He's right wound up about it. Says 'e's come back."

Steve was shocked to the core by Kevin's announcement. Surely they couldn't be talking about the same ghost? He feigned insouciance.

"What d'you mean, come back?" Like a ghost? That old man's losing it."

Kevin shot to his feet and lifted a threatening fist. "No he isn't! 'E told me all about it, how one of 'is mates got killed way back, an' how 'e keeps thinking that 'e's come back!"

Steve took a step back, as surprised by the vehemence of Kevin's reaction as his revelation.

"Steady on, mate," Steve held his hands out in front of him in a conciliatory gesture. "I didn't mean anything by it, but you don't hear about ghosts every day, do you? I mean, if I told you that I'd seen one, what would you say?"

"Sorry, Steve," mumbled Kevin. "The old man's really cut up about it."

Steve realised that Kevin, probably without knowing it, had more respect for George Williams than anybody else. Kevin never talked about his family, and it dawned on Steve that he may not have any close relatives and had latched on to George as a sort of surrogate father figure.

Dark spots suddenly began to appear on the table between them, and Steve, his curiosity aroused as never before, suggested that the two of them went inside for a drink. Kevin, broke as usual, agreed to just the one, if Steve was buying. Checking the contents of his wallet, Steve agreed, and they headed inside just as the heavens opened.

***

The rain was drumming on the roof of Jack Rimmer's hire car as he searched for a parking space close to the Mellings' flat. Finding a small gap outside a motorcycle dealer on the corner of Stricklands Lane, he carefully manoeuvred the Nissan Micra into the opening. Waiting for the shower to pass overhead, he observed a woman in her forties emerge from the front door of Katie and Steve's building. Putting up an umbrella, she turned and waved towards the uppermost floor of the flats before huddling under the floral canopy and half running along the road. As she turned the corner into Leyland Road, Jack decided that he would brave the downpour after all.

Taking his briefcase, he held it over his head as he ran through the deluge, splashing in a puddle and soaking his left foot as he reached the opposite kerb. Muttering obscenities under his breath, he chastised himself for not looking where he was going in the knowledge that his foot would probably be wet and uncomfortable until he could return to the hotel. He had returned to see Katie on the off-chance that she had had another visitation and thereby gleaned more information.

As it turned out, his optimism had been misplaced.

"My mother's only just left," Katie informed him. "Our visitor only seems to appear when it's just us here. He must be shy, or something."

Katie was as surprised as Jack at her nonchalant attitude to what he thought must have been a terrifying experience. In fact, she had sensed the return of the spectre as her mother had closed the door behind her, only for the feeling to quickly dissipate. Jack's appearance a few moments later had gone some way to explaining the reason for the apparition's seeming change of heart.

"Steve will be home soon. Why don't you stay for a while? I'm sure that he would like to meet you. Tea?" Katie headed into the kitchen as Jack nodded his assent.

"Go into the living room and make yourself at home." she called. Jack picked his way through the minefield of Fisher Price toys and joined Joshua in the small room at the front of the flat. The toddler looked up from his endeavours with a plastic hammer, stared blankly at Jack for a moment, then returned to his impact engineering.

About half an hour later, Steve arrived, apologising to his wife for being late. Jack recognised him from their brief encounter in the road outside the previous week, but Steve's reaction was somewhat different. Picking up his son, who had flung himself at his father as soon as he entered the room, Steve fixed Jack with a meaningful stare.

"You look just like him. Do you know that?" Jack was lost for words, and Steve continued regardless. "I think that I know what happened. What's more, one of the men responsible lives just the other side of the river."

"His name is George Williams. He used to be on the railway, as a signalman, I think." Steve began to recount the information that he had gleaned from his encounter with Kevin Anderson. "I've known him for ages: he drinks at the Labour club. He has some weird ideas about how society should work, but he's an interesting guy none the less.

"Anyway, Kevin is pretty close to him, and spends time at George's house. It turns out that George has been seeing ghosts too, not as close as we have, but, according to Kevin, he knows who it is and how he died."

Something about the name made Jack reach for his briefcase. Rummaging through the papers and notes jumbled together inside, he finally found what he was looking for.

"Was he involved in derailing a munitions train?" Jack's voice was sombre yet commanding; another vestige of his military career.

"Yeah, that's him. How did you know?" Steve asked as Katie looked on, not comprehending.

"It's all here, from the Public Records Office. I found a declassified MI5 report from nineteen forty-one. The name George Williams appears as one of a group of Communist sympathisers who were fooled into attacking the train by a German spy."

"German? Kevin said that they were helped by a 'comrade'. They thought that they were working for the Russians! Do you think that they ever knew the truth?" Steve's mouth opened and closed briefly, but no more words came. A brief silence ensued, broken by Katie's somewhat indignant voice.

"Will one of you tell me what is going on?"

Jack took a deep breath. "Until July forty-one the Germans and Russians had a non-aggression pact. They had carved up Poland between them and the Russians had defeated the Finns the previous winter. The British government had supplied arms to the Finns before the war began so, in the eyes of some, Britain was at war with Germany *and* the Soviet Union.

"That was never the case, of course, but some people with Communist sympathies were prepared to disrupt the war effort. It was never official Party policy, but small acts of mostly industrial sabotage were carried out. According to the official record at least some of this sabotage was encouraged by an agent codenamed 'Sciron' who claimed to be a Soviet spy.

"His real name was never known, but MI5 found out that he was in fact working for the Abwehr, which was the German's secret service. So these people weren't working for the Russians at all. In April of that year, George Williams and two accomplices, having failed to stop a munitions train by blocking the line to the docks, were encouraged to try again by derailing the train before it got to the goods station at the bottom of Fishergate Hill."

A howl of pain interrupted Jack's lecture. Joshua had managed to hammer his own thumb and ran to his mother in floods of tears.

"I'd best put him to bed," Katie picked up the toddler and hugged him. "Back in a few minutes."

"You got all that from that piece of paper?" Steve was clearly impressed.

"Not all of it. The man who wrote this report lives in Sussex. I'd interviewed him before for another book."

"How many books have you written, then? What are they called?" He wasn't actually a fan of the written word, vastly preferring his entertainment to be largely visual. But Steve Melling had never met a real live author before and was determined to have something to tell his work mates the next day.

"Six in total, and unless you are a serious student of military history I can guarantee that you won't have heard of any of them."

"Oh. Still, this will make a good book then, won't it?"

"It would, if I thought that anybody would believe it."

***

The evening's heavy showers had cleared the air, and the smell of damp grass pervaded as George Williams locked his front door and crossed the road toward the riverbank. He had intended to make his way to the club to relieve his unremitting loneliness, but this evening he found himself drawn across the river towards the man-made embankment that had once been part of his railway.

On the south bank, a pathway, marked for both pedestrians and cyclists, followed the line of the old railway at the bottom of the bank. As George walked, to his left mature trees towered over him casting the former alignment into deep shadow. Occasional drops of water lost their grip on the young leaves and splattered on and around the old man as he strode on, his flat cap pulled down on his head and his hands thrust in his pockets to evade the twilight chill. Crossing Leyland Road, he picked up the path again as it squeezed between a redundant bridge abutment and the Methodist Church.

As the breeze ruffled the branches above him, George suddenly felt utterly wretched. A heartbeat later, he thought that heard somebody's voice.

It's time... others are coming...why did you do it?

George's head snapped to the left and up towards the top of

the bank next to him. Fear gripped him, instantly replacing the despondent feeling despite that fact that there was nobody to be seen. Turning on his heel, he quickened his pace, not pausing until he was back on the main road.

Fighting for breath, he sat on the low wall surrounding the front of the church. Sweat poured from his brow as his eyes frantically scanned the embankment for any sign of pursuit. Again, the feeling of sheer misery began to envelop him and he pressed his hands against his ears in a vain attempt to keep out the voice.

Others are coming...

***

Joshua's distress had proven to be a lengthy affair. After forty-five minutes, with no change to the intensity of the infantile anguish, Jack had made his excuses and left the Mellings to comfort their son. Returning to the hotel, he decided once again to gather his thoughts in the pub rather than in the solitude of his room.

As with the previous Tuesday night, the bar was virtually deserted. Remembering that the house wine was quite passable, he ordered a large glass of red from the obviously bored and uncommunicative girl behind the bar. As she shuffled off to get his drink, Jack's mobile phone rang. At the sound of the Nokia tune (Jack had never figured out how to change it), the few faces in the room turned to look at him, causing him to flush with embarrassment. He quickly removed it from his jacket pocket and stabbed at the green button with his index finger.

"Jack Rimmer."

A familiar female voice came back. "Hello, Jack. It's Janice Forsyth."

Jack was momentarily lost for words.

"Jack, are you there?"

"Yes...yes of course. How nice to hear from you, Janice. Sorry, you took me by surprise. Hold on a moment."

His drink had arrived. Jack pulled a five pound note from his wallet and handed it to the girl, then turned and made his way to a corner table without waiting for his change.

"Sorry about that. Now, what can I do for you?" Jack was hoping that this was a purely social call, but Janice's tone of voice suggested otherwise.

"Are you still researching your father's death?"

"Yes, I am. I'm in Lancashire at the moment but I should be back by..." Janice cut him off before he could explain.

"My father wants to meet with you again. In Preston. I've no idea why, and I'm not happy with him travelling all that way. He won't admit it, but he's really quite frail."

"Do you know what he wants?" Jack was intrigued, not only at the thought of something so important that Cedric Morgan wanted to travel well over two hundred miles to talk about it, but also at the possibility that his daughter may accompany him.

At the other end, Janice sighed. "I've no idea, Jack. But he insists that he must come to you, not the other way around. I shall have to drive him, of course."

Jack's heart leapt. "When will you come? Do you want me to arrange some accommodation for you? When..." He realised that he was jabbering excitedly.

"He wants to come straight away, so we'll set off tomorrow. And yes, would you please find us somewhere to stay?"

"Of course. I'll ring you in the morning and let you know where."

Their conversation ended, Jack returned the phone to his pocket and drank deeply from his glass. It took him a moment to realise it, but he was grinning to himself. Silly old fool, he thought. But once again a mental image of Janice prevented him from concentrating on the job at hand. Jack had meant to spend at least an hour writing up a summary of what he knew in an attempt to identify the gaps in his knowledge, but it took a considerable effort of will to finish his drink and return to his room and his waiting laptop.

***

As Jack was answering his phone, Katie Melling was still trying to calm her son. Steve had tried, but Joshua was something of a mummy's boy and had simply shrieked still louder. Tiring of walking around in the confines of the flat, she had sat on her bed with Joshua sat on her lap. Suddenly, he stopped crying and looked towards the door. As he did so, Katie sensed the approach of their spectral visitor; however, the feeling was less of sadness and more of fear tinged with menace.

"Man coming," said Joshua and buried his face in Katie's chest. Steve came through the door, a nervous expression on his face.

"It's him again, isn't it?" He paused, seeing the wide-eyed look on his wife's face.

"There's something different this time," she said. "It always felt sad before, but now it's...it's...scary." A shiver ran down her spine as she spoke, the involuntary spasm making the little boy begin to whimper again.

The sensation grew in intensity until it seemed to fill the air around them. Steve sat on the bed next to Katie and put him arm around her shoulder, almost at once realising the futility of his action. For the first time, their perception of the apparition's approach was more than their imagination: simultaneously Steve and Katie both realised that a tangible odour was present in the room.

"Do you smell that?" asked Katie. "What is it?"

"Smells like... oh, I don't know...is it the river? It's certainly sort of damp, don't you think?"

"Men coming!" sobbed Joshua, clinging still closer to his mother.

Steve and Katie looked at each other, the apprehension apparent on both their faces. Katie was trembling now and Steve pulled her closer to him. His own insides were knotted with fear and the shame that he could not protect his family from the horror that approached.

As they both looked back towards the door, a familiar figure appeared in front of them. He, at least was unchanged: the dejected expression held no malice. The spectre stood in the doorway looking at them, then half turned to look over his shoulder. When he looked back, the voiceless words came to Steve and Katie again.

The others are coming...it's almost time.

"What others, Jack?" It was Katie that had spoken, adding to Steve's shame. "What's happening?"

He will be here...the others are coming to meet him.

"Do they want to hurt us, Jack? Have we done something?"

They want him...the one that sent us to...

His sentence unfinished, the apparition turned again. A sudden cacophony of voices filled the heads of the couple perched on the edge of the bed; the words were blurred, indistinct, like a crowd of people all shouting at once. The ghost turned back and faced them.

Tell him...we are waiting for him...he will answer for what he has done.

Wednesday Morning

Jack Rimmer had risen early. Despite a late night collating the information that he had gleaned from each source, he felt quite fresh. He shaved carefully, showered, then went to the reception desk to enquire about two additional rooms. Having secured these using his own credit card, he returned to the restaurant in the pub next door and treated himself to a full English breakfast.

Returning to his room, Jack looked afresh at the holes in his knowledge. He was certain that his father had been killed by a blow to the head somewhere close to where the Mellings' flat now stood. From what he had learned the previous day, the prime suspect was George Williams, spurred on by the spy Sciron. But there were still some questions. Why had his father left the security of his signal box? Why had his disappearance not been investigated? It occurred to Jack that he didn't know where his father's remains were now, having been discovered recently. And why did Cedric Morgan want to travel the length of the country to see him in Preston?

It was that thought, and the accompanying image of Janice, that reminded Jack that he hadn't phoned to let them know where the hotel was. Taking out his mobile phone, he looked at the last received call (he wasn't completely technophobic) and pressed the green handset button to dial the number. To his disappointment, Morgan himself answered the phone.

"Oh, it's you, Rimmer," Cedric's voice was subdued, hesitant. "Janice is driving. Give me the details would you, old chap."

Jack passed on the hotel's address and some brief instructions how to find it.

"It's relatively simple, just off junction 29 of the motorway. I've booked two rooms."

"Thank you, Rimmer. We'll be up there at about two this afternoon, so Janice tells me. Will you be around then?"

Wild horses wouldn't drag me away, thought Jack. But he confined his response to a simple "of course" before hanging up. The tone of Morgan's voice was a little disturbing, he thought a moment later, quite out of character. These thoughts were soon suppressed by the rising excitement at the prospect of seeing Janice once more, in spite of his best efforts to curb his juvenile enthusiasm. Smiling to himself, he shook his head and returned to his laptop.

He had to speak to George Williams; that much was certain. Jack was dreading the encounter: what would he say? 'Hello, Mr Williams, did you kill my father?' or 'My name's Jack Rimmer. You orphaned me'. No, he needed a more subtle approach.

Looking at his list of questions, Jack realised that Steve's recounting of Kevin Anderson's story held the clue. Williams had been a signalman, just like his father. That would be his approach: he needed to know why his father had left his post and Williams could probably give him that answer to that.

Looking at an online telephone directory, there were thirteen 'G Williams' shown in Preston. On a hunch, Jack phoned Katie Melling, hoping that Steve would still be there. He was in luck.

"I don't know the house number," said the younger man, "but I do know that he lives just over the river from us on Broadgate."

Thanking Steve, Jack hung up before he could be informed of the previous night's development. Jack looked again at the directory. Sure enough, just one 'G Williams'. He paused for a moment, briefly mentally rehearsing his cover story. Then he dialled the number.

I'm too old for this, thought Janice Forsyth, becoming restive at being stuck in yet another seemingly endless line of slow-moving traffic. They had made poor progress since she had collected her father from his cottage; now, on their third different motorway she realised that it had taken three hours to cover just eighty miles or so. Her car didn't help: a Peugeot 106 was not built for long journeys or high speeds, not that the latter was a problem today.

Strangely, the call from Jack Rimmer had helped. Just as she was considering surrendering herself to the encompassing embrace of uncontrolled road rage, her father's conversation had diverted her attention sufficiently to assuage her rising anger. For, like Jack, she had felt an attraction between them. It was an odd feeling, the resurgence of a long-forgotten sensation that she had considered consigned to history. Like Jack, she thought that she must be past such juvenile emotion and, like Jack, felt just a little foolish at the possibility of starting a relationship with a man whom she hardly knew and, as a life-long bachelor, would hardly be interested in an elderly widow.

Yet she didn't actually feel like an elderly widow. She had retired early, but not *that* early, from teaching to nurse her husband through the cancer that would take him from her. She was now sixty-six, but in her heart she felt no different to when she was in her thirties, with three young children, a secure career and a successful husband. She had met Paul at university: he was in his final year studying architecture when she had begun her English course. They had married as soon as she graduated aged twenty-two and within eight years their family had grown with the addition of two boys and a girl. They were grown up themselves now, with families of their own, and it had been the grandchildren that had helped Janice through the dark days following Paul's death.

She had had male friends since then, but could never bring herself to commit to a relationship with any of them. None of them had stayed in her life for long: whereas she wanted companionship, they wanted sex, and none were prepared to wait until she was ready. Paul had been her only lover: on the rare occasion she had come close to going to bed with another man the feeling that she was betraying her dead husband had been strong enough to prevent her going through with it.

But this new sensation was different to the others. Previously, the men had pursued her, now she felt that she might be the one to make the running. Yes, maybe Jack was the one that would share her dotage, and, before that, her bed.

The impatient blaring of a car horn snapped her out of her trance. The traffic ahead of her had moved a whole hundred yards and the man in the vehicle behind was clearly as fed up as she had been just moments earlier.

"Do pay attention, Janice," muttered Cedric, grumpily. "I'd like to get there today, if possible." Smiling to herself, Janice put the car in gear, released the handbrake and closed up the gap.

***

The phone had rung countless times, and Jack was on the verge of hanging up when a gruff voice finally answered.

"Is that Mr George Williams?" asked Jack, his voice as affable as he could manage.

"Yes. What do you want? I'm not interested in buying anything!" George virtually shouted back at his caller.

"Mr Williams, my name is Jack...er...Melling," Jack knew that his genuine surname might have spooked the old man, and used the first one that came into his head. "I'm an historian, and I am researching a book on the relationship between the trade union movement and the railways."

"Go on," George's tone betrayed his sudden interest, but he was still suspicious. "Who put you on to me?"

"I have interviewed several people in this area, and your name seems to crop up more than anybody else. Apparently you were quite active in the movement. Could I possibly call round to speak to you? When would suit?" Dissimulation did not come easy to Jack, and keeping his tenor even was proving a strain.

"I'm not going anywhere. Come round now, if you want." His mood had obviously lightened at the thought that he might still be remembered on the railway. It had never occurred to him that people might not have even slightly positive memories of him: he was too sure of his own righteousness for that.

"Thank you, I will. See you in about half an hour." Jack hung up.

Thirty-five minutes later he was standing outside George Williams' front door, feeling very nervous. Swallowing hard, he rapped loudly on the wooden panel and took a step back. For what seemed like an eternity, he waited for the door to open. When it finally did, the old man before him did an immediate double-take. His rheumy eyes narrowed, and he gave Jack a look that conveyed both hostility and fear at the same time.

"Who are you?" he growled, and, without waiting for an answer, started to close the door.

Jack managed to get his foot in the door before it slammed, causing him to grit his teeth in pain. "Mr Williams, it's Jack Melling. I phoned you just before. Please let me in!"

"Melling, you say? I know a Melling, a young fella. You look like someone else." There was uncertainty in the old man's words, and he opened the door again. "You look just like somebody I used to know. Was your father a railwayman?"

"As a matter of fact, he was. Could we talk about it inside?" George reluctantly stepped back and gestured for him to enter. Jack did so, trying not to limp too obviously despite the throbbing from his foot. Pausing in the hallway, he waited for George to lead the way into his front room. The older man sat heavily in his chair and waved vaguely towards the other seat where Kevin Anderson had sat previously.

"Yes," said Jack, summoning up all the courage that he could muster."My father was a signalman, his name was Jack Rimmer, and I think that you killed him."

***

Mike Simpson was back at work, once again employing his new-found talent for looking busy whilst cogitating over his next move. The lack of nocturnal visits from, well, whoever it was, suggested that he must be on the right lines. He had spent some time the previous evening looking at the Penwortham Triangle, or what remained of it, on Google Earth. He had been struck by the revelation that disused railways stand out on aerial photographs as well as, if not better than, existing ones; he had also noticed that one point of the triangle had been replaced by a small housing estate. But it still didn't tell him what he was supposed to do. Without really knowing why, he had used another website to print a map of the area and a route from the railway station. He had also checked train times to Preston: the journey was a long one but at least there were direct trains. Mike was not an experienced traveller and the prospect of having to change trains, even once, put him off attempting most journeys.

One of his co-workers, a plain and somewhat overweight girl of nineteen, came over to where he was absent-mindedly polishing the same table that had been the object of his attention for the past five minutes.

"Mike, can you help me in the back? There's a funny smell and I can't figure out what it is." She pushed her over-sized glasses up her nose as she spoke. She was very short-sighted, and the glasses made her eyes look large and slightly out of focus.

"Err...OK. I'll be there in a moment" said Mike, trying, with reasonable success, to hide his annoyance at being disturbed.

Walking to the back of the shop, a familiar odour wafted into his nostrils. A clammy, humid ambience, just like in his bedroom during one of the visitations, hung in the air. The feeling of hatred that had accompanied the appearance of the spectres was there too: diminished, but still palpable.

"I think it might be the drain back here" he shouted over his shoulder. "I'll see to it. You cover the shop." The girl, like Mike not the most diligent of employees, was happy to leave the job to him and pulled the door closed as she fixed the next customer with her slightly odd stare.

Mike realised that he was trembling slightly. Looking around the room, he sensed a presence but couldn't see anything. Just then, a shadow flickered in the corner of his right eye, the movement attracting his attention. He snapped his head to the right, but there was nothing to be seen.

"Are you there?" he hissed in a hoarse whisper, immediately feeling somewhat foolish.

You must go there.

Mike's head turned left and right, his frantic gaze hunting for the shadowy figure that he knew was there but that evaded his searching.

He is approaching.

"What do you want me to do? I don't know anything about this!" whispered Mike, not knowing in which direction to address his words.

Just be there. You will know what to do.

***

Katie Melling was having a bad day. She had slept poorly; a combination of her unborn child's constant squirming, Steve's snoring and the fear created by "the others" had conspired to prevent what passed for a restful night in her present condition. Joshua, as if sensing her tiredness and determined to exploit it to the full, had been a recalcitrant handful. He had refused to eat his breakfast, then fought her when she tried to dress him. He clung to her every step, constantly crying and begging to be picked up.

Her nerves frayed beyond reason, Katie tried once again to

calm him down, but to no avail. His little face was a picture of anguish, the effect comically mitigated by the constant stream from his nose. Several soggy tissues were strewn around the flat as his mother vainly sought to stem the flow. The final straw had been the orange juice. Demanding a drink, Joshua had insisted on sitting on her knee in the living room as he lifted the plastic beaker: when he spilled the bulk of the contents they had poured down himself, Katie's last clean maternity dress and thence on to the carpet, where it formed a sticky damp patch.

Katie could take no more. Bursting into tears of frustration herself, she reached for the phone to call her mother. To add insult to injury, there was no reply: her mother used Katie's day off work to do her main shopping and Katie wept all the more with the realisation of that fact.

After a moment, she realised that Joshua had stopped crying. Instead, he was sat, transfixed, his eyes wide.

"Mummy, don't like," he virtually whimpered the words. "Make nasty people go away, Mummy!" With that, he buried his head in her bosom and clutched at her dress, pulling himself tight against her. Katie soon realised why: the ghost was returning, and he was not alone. The familiar feeling of misery was swamped by bitterness, menace and hatred so intense that it made the blood drain from her face.

Wrapping her arms around her son, Katie looked left and right, unable to see the apparition. Terror gripped her very being in a way that even the first appearance of Jack Rimmer Senior had not achieved. Again, she looked around her, the rapid movement of her head making her pony tail swing around on to Joshua's head. He stayed stock still, despite the uncontrolled trembling of his mother.

"Jack! Where are you?" screamed Katie, near to hysteria."Show yourself, please! What is happening?"

Tears were streaming down her face now, her fear multiplying with the escalating sensation of danger and loathing that was now permeating the air. The musty, damp smell had returned, incongruously reminding Katie of the beach holidays in North Wales she had enjoyed with her parents before the untimely death of her father. Why can't *he* haunt me, she thought, at least he would never frighten me this way.

The uninvited memories of her father added residual grief to the dread that she felt. She was about to cry out again when a bright light filled the hallway beyond the living room door. Silhouetted in the doorway was the figure of the elder Rimmer, his back to her and his arms held wide.

The one that you seek is not here...leave her...she can help you.

With this, the spectre turned to face Katie. As he did so, she could see behind him the outlines of other people and could hear them babbling incoherently.

You must bring him to us...the time of reckoning is close...bring the one that condemned us to drown...only he can give us peace.

"Who are you talking about?" pleaded Katie. "Tell me, who is he? What do you want with him?"

He is coming...he must atone...we must have justice!

Wednesday Afternoon

Above the southern Labrador Sea, an unseasonably deep depression was wrapping active weather fronts around its centre. The warm front, marked by lowering cloud and gradually increasing rainfall, was being chased by a cold front which had already formed towering cumulus clouds that brought sharp deluges interspersed with deceptive sunny spells. On the weather charts at the Meteorological Office, the tightly packed isobars, lines of equal atmospheric pressure, told a tale of gale force winds. Reports from ships in the area told of falling barometers: the winds were set to increase to storm force. Warned by long-wave radio reports, vessels in the North Atlantic were scurrying for shelter, running from the towering waves, driven ever higher by the howling tempest.

Higher still, the Jet stream, the ribbon of winds blowing at up to two hundred miles per hour, steered the maelstrom eastwards, towards Iceland and the British Isles.

These facts, completely unbeknown to Janice Forsyth, would not have helped the ennui that was accompanied by cramp in her left foot and a dull ache that was spreading upwards from the small of her back. The journey was an endless miasma of tarmac and concrete, broken only by a single stop at a service station for expensive coffee and over-priced petrol. Hours had passed: the M1 had given way to the M6 virtually unnoticed. As the miles clocked by, the atmosphere in the car became more strained. Cedric had sat, silent, staring out of the windscreen, occasionally speaking only to criticise his daughter's driving.

Janice had tried switching on the radio, only to have her father crossly turn it off again without so much as a word. That had been somewhere near Coventry; now, having negotiated the permanent tailback past Birmingham, they were moving at a reasonable speed once more through Staffordshire and into Cheshire. It seemed that the further north they travelled, the more her father's mood blackened. Finally, a full seven hours after leaving Sussex, she espied a sign giving fifty-five miles to Preston. Less than an hour to go: her relief was palpable. She mentioned as much to Cedric, only to be met with little more than a grunt.

Janice could not help but feel a little frisson of excitement at her proximity to Jack. Once again, she attempted to curb her enthusiasm by reminding herself that Jack had shown no outward sign of interest in her; once again, she smiled inwardly at the thought of being close to him once more.

The last hour of the journey seemed interminable. Another traffic jam leading up to the Thelwall Viaduct had merged with yet another caused by an accident further north, delaying them by an additional twenty minutes. Finally, the junction that they were seeking came into view, Cedric guided her using Jack's directions, and just a few moments later they were parked outside the hotel.

Janice extracted herself from the car, straightening up slowly as her back protested at the abuse. Finally achieving an upright posture, she noticed that her father was still sitting in the car.

"Come on. Dad," she pleaded, trying to keep a note of exasperation out of her voice. "We're here. Let's get inside."

Moving to the back of the car, she lifted the hatch to retrieve their luggage. Taking the two bags out and slamming the lid closed, she was angered by her father's lack of movement. Dropping the bags, she strode to the passenger door and yanked it open.

"Dad, stop messing about and..." her words caught in her mouth. Cedric was sat, still staring forward, but tears were streaming from his eyes.

"I'm sorry, my dear, but I'm afraid that I'm going to be an awful disappointment to you."

***

"My name's Rimmer, not Melling. My father, as I said, was Jack Rimmer. Ring any bells?"

Jack fixed the older man with what he hoped was an icy glare, despite the fear he felt inside. George Williams was stunned into silence for a moment, his mouth half open but his eyes blazing. His face flushed and he began to struggle to his feet, making it half way out of the chair before stopping momentarily then collapsing back into it. When he spoke, his voice was soft; sorrowful instead of the anger that Jack was expecting.

"It wasn't me."

"But I have it on good authority..." Jack was bluffing, but George brusquely cut him off.

"It wasn't me! Shut up and listen! I've been waiting sixty-five years to tell this story, so just keep quiet!" He paused for a moment to gather his thoughts. Jack remained silent, but surreptitiously slipped his right hand into his jacket pocket and, feeling with his thumb for the appropriate switch, set his digital recorder to capture the story.

"There were four of us. Me, Bill Farebrother and George Peters were railwaymen and the other one was, well, he was a spy. Never knew his name: he called himself Sky-something."

"Sciron, by any chance?" interrupted Jack, gently.

"That's him. How did you...oh, never mind. Anyway, we were all Communists. I still am, as it happens. We decided that since the Germans and the Soviets were allies, we would do whatever we could to disrupt the war effort. We hated Hitler, of course, but we trusted Comrade Stalin. Sciron started turning up at union and Party meetings, and after a few weeks he asked me whether I would help with some more direct action, as he put it.

"I asked him what he meant, and he told me to meet him in a

pub down by the docks the next night. There, he told me that the British government were going to send arms and ammunition to Finland, to spark off another war with the Soviet Union, and did I want to help stop it? Well, of course I did. I had no loyalty to the capitalist bourgeoisie of England, did I? Anyway, there was a ship coming into Preston docks, and a train load of ammunition was supposed to meet it. We knew that we couldn't get anywhere near the docks, they were too well guarded. So we decided to blow up the railway to the docks. Sciron had a suitcase full of explosives, and between the three of us railwaymen, we knew where they would work best.

"So we took them to the mouth of the tunnel where the line comes down from Preston station. We set the charges on the track and in the tunnel, then disappeared, sharpish. The explosives worked fine: the line was blocked for a week. Trouble was, there was another Preston station in those days, much closer to the docks, at the bottom of Fishergate Hill. It was the old West Lancashire Railway terminus, and had been closed to passengers for about ten years by then. I found out that the train that we had stopped was going to that station instead, to be unloaded by soldiers on to trucks.

"I called round at Bill and George's houses, told them, and we sat by the river trying to think what we could do next. It was Bill's idea, I think, to derail the train before it could get to the station, so we arranged to meet up after I finished my shift in Penwortham Junction signal box, down at the old Middleforth Junction. There was a bridge there, over Stricklands Lane. We didn't have much time before the train was due, so I went up the pole route to cut the block lines."

"I'm sorry, the *what* lines? What's a pole route?" Jack interjected, not having the faintest idea what George was talking about.

George sighed heavily. "Ever wondered why a train has a red light on the back? Well, in the old mechanical signal boxes, we kept the trains apart using a system called Absolute Block. In simple terms, we wouldn't let a train on to the bit of line between the signal boxes unless we had seen the tail lamp of the train before go past us. That way we knew that the train was complete when it had passed and hadn't left a wagon or carriage blocking the line. With me so far?"

Jack nodded, hoping that his recorder was getting all this.

"So, rather than ring the next signal box each time we wanted to pass a train through, we used a device called a block instrument, which had a Morse key on it to make bell signals, a switch so that we could say that our bit of line was clear or had a train in it, and an indicator to give us the same information from the next box. These devices were connected by wires than ran between telegraph poles, called the pole route. So, I climbed one of the telegraph poles to cut the wires between the signal boxes. Now do you understand?"

"Yes...yes, I think so. But why did my father leave his signal box?"

"Probably because I cut the wrong wires. I realised when I had climbed down, but I hadn't cut the block wires at all. I'm not sure to this day what I did cut, but I do know that it was enough to get Jack walking down towards us. I had gone back up the pole when he arrived, but the others were loosening rails. Sciron had turned up: he must have been following us."

"So, if you were up the pole, who killed my father?" demanded Jack, failing to keep a rising nervousness, verging on desperation, out of his voice.

"Sciron."

***

"J...justice?" The fear in Katie's voice was manifest. She was still sat on the settee, clutching Joshua to her. Her son was sobbing now, his tears leaving a dark stain on Katie's t-shirt. She was virtually paralysed with terror: her only movement the uncontrollable shaking that make her voice quake. The spectre had once again turned his back to her, blocking the way for the ghostly figures that appeared to be lurking in her hallway. They were quiet now, but the sense of unbridled hatred still permeated the room. If anything, their silence was more menacing than the tumult of before.

Bring him to us...give us peace.

"Bring who? I don't know who you want!" pleaded Katie.

He is near now...bring him...my son will help.

"I'll try! I promise, I really will try! Now, please, make them go away!"

The light in the doorway began to subside and with it the sense of dampness and the atmosphere of loathing. Rimmer's ghost remained for a moment, then turned and looked at the wretched figure sat shivering before him. Her eyes, red now, appeared to beg him to spare her any more of this torment. Her tear-streaked face was a picture of abject terror and the small boy clinging to her was petrified with fright.

Sorry...they will come again; soon...you must bring him to us.

"But I don't know who he is," muttered Katie, unable to raise more than a hoarse whisper. "How can I bring him if I don't know who you want? Why can't..." Her voice tailed off as she realised that she was once again alone with her son. Joshua's head came up; his hand found his mother's face and gently turned her head so that she looked at him. His face was expressionless, uncomprehending. For a few seconds they sat staring at each other, then the mood was broken by the little boy opening his mouth in a gaping yawn and his balled fists rubbing his eyes.

Katie regained sufficient self-control to struggle to her feet, still holding Joshua, and heading for his bedroom. She paused at the living room door, suddenly nervous of her own hallway. Then, summoning up her last reserves of mental strength, she stepped into the small space and on towards Joshua's bedroom. He already had his head on her shoulder, his breathing slower and deeper as he succumbed to his tiredness. By the time that Katie had laid him softly in his cot, he was fast asleep. Carefully covering him, she kissed her finger and touched it against his face, then turned and left the room.

Making her way, robot-like, into the kitchen, Katie filled the kettle without really being conscious of her actions. She reached up into the cupboard for a clean mug, but it slipped from her fingers and shattered on the worktop in front of her. Staring mutely at the broken china for a couple of seconds, she could contain her emotions no longer. Angrily sweeping the ceramic shards on to the floor with her hand, she burst into tears once more: not the silent weeping of previously, but an anguished, fervent lament.

As she stood, leaning on the worktop, head bowed, the tears ran down and dripped from the end of her nose, forming a pool on the surface in front of her. Transfixed by distress, she stared at the tiny puddle. Without warning, a sharp pain seared across her back.

"Oh, no...NO! Not now!"

***

Janice stood, shocked by the sight of her father in tears. He had always been one of the old school: outward displays of emotion were anathema to him. She had certainly never seen him cry before, even after the death of her mother. Now he was sat in the front seat of her car, his shoulders shaking and his breath coming in short sobs, seemingly unable to say anything more. She felt a tear welling up in her own eye, and dropped on to one knee to address him.

"Dad, what on earth is it? I've never seen you in such a state!" Her words seemed to help him to regain some of his composure; his breathing became more regular and he blinked to clear his eyes.

"Janice, my dear, the next day or so is going to be very difficult for both of us. Do you have a tissue? Thank you." Cedric dabbed his eyes and dried his cheeks. "Please, go inside and check us in, while I try to make myself presentable."

"But what is all this about?" The concern in his daughter's voice caused Cedric to finally turn and look her in the eye.

"All in good time, Janice. All in good time. Now, please, do as I ask and sort out our rooms, would you. I'll be in momentarily"

Without another word, Janice looked at him for a second or two before rising to her feet and moving to the back of the car. Extracting the folding handles from the two small suitcases, she took one in each hand and began towing them in the direction of the hotel reception. Half way to the door, she looked back, but Cedric gestured her inside with a dismissive wave of his hand. Once inside, Janice went up to the reception desk, only to find it deserted. Unable to find a call button or a bell, she called out.

"Hello! Can somebody help me?"

A young woman put her head around the door of the office behind the desk. She had a telephone handset in her hand.

"Just a mo and I'll be with you." She gestured towards the handset, as if Janice couldn't guess what she was doing, and disappeared once more.

Janice stretched her back and looked around the hotel foyer. It was functional, utilitarian, with a low leather two seat settee either side of a glass coffee table as the only furniture. She could hear snatches of the receptionist's conversation: she was clearly arranging to meet up with somebody after work. This annoyed Janice; she would never have considered keeping a client waiting whilst making a personal call. She was about to attract the woman's attention once more when a familiar figure came through the front door.

"Jack! I wasn't expecting to see you quite so soon." The jollity in her voice belied her discomfort at seeing him before she had had a chance to freshen up. Her hair felt lank, she had no make-up on and, having been sat in the car for hours, she was sure that she must be in need of a dab of perfume.

Jack Rimmer looked at her. She was wearing a tight-fitting black polo-neck sweater and jeans tucked into calf-length suede boots. She thought that she was a mess: he thought that she looked stunning. He was reminded of Orsino's line in the final act of Twelfth Night: "Here comes the Countess: now heaven walks on earth."

"Hello, Janice," he said, feigning an indifference that disguised his delight in seeing her again. "Where's Cedric?"

"He'll be along in a moment. He's...er...fetching something from the car." They stood, about six feet apart, just looking into each other's eyes without either of them having the faintest idea what to say next. The awkwardness of the moment was broken by the receptionist, who had finally deigned to attend to her customers.

"Shall we have dinner?" asked Jack, the formalities completed. "About eight o'clock?"

"I'd love to," she replied, wondering what she was going to do for the three hours until then. Getting ready wouldn't take *that* long. "I'll see what Dad wants to do."

"I was hoping it would be just us, if that's acceptable?" said Jack, desperately keeping a pleading tone out of his voice.

Her heart leapt. "That would be lovely."

Wednesday Evening

Mike Simpson returned home after his shift, having firstly arranged to have a couple of days off and secondly withdrawn a substantial proportion of his bank balance. Despite his minimum-wage earnings, the fact that he never went out and, until that week, had been living for free meant that he actually had over four hundred pounds in his current account. He had taken two hundred and fifty: the maximum that his bank would allow in a single day. Still not knowing what role in the ghostly exposition he was playing, he was nonetheless determined to catch the first train to Preston the next morning. What he would do from there, he had no idea: he was relying wholly on spectral inspiration when he arrived at the Penwortham Triangle.

Pushing open the front door to their pebble-dashed semi, he put his head around the door of the living room, only to be waved away by his mother. She was sat with her friend Karen, and, despite the early hour, they were on their second bottle of Blue Nun. A gloomy Karen had turned up some forty-five minutes earlier, seeking a sympathetic ear from her best friend. Her night of passion the previous Friday had been a sordid affair; not so much sexual fervour than a re-enactment of some pornographic movie which left her feeling exploited. That feeling had quickly given way to disgust, largely with herself, followed by a deep shame. Feeling dirty and violated, she had sat on her bed and cried for the best part of an hour before running a hot bath and soaking in it for even longer. It had taken her five days to pluck up the courage to talk to anybody about it; now she was sat on the settee with her head on her friend's shoulder with tears running down her cheeks once more.

Oblivious to all of this, Mike went to his bedroom to check the train times to Preston. The National Railways website told him that the first train was at a quarter past six. Perhaps the second train, thought Mike. That left just after seven, arriving in Preston at half past nine. That one would do. Sensing a presence behind him, he turned around, expecting to be faced by a dripping spectre. He was almost disappointed when he saw his mother standing in the doorway.

"Can you sort your own tea out tonight, love?" she whispered. "Karen's feeling a bit depressed. Here's a fiver, why not go to the chippy?"

"Yeah, OK, Mum. Can I just have a quick word, though?"

A quizzical expression came across her face. "Can't it wait until later?"

"Not really. You see, I'm taking a couple of days off work. I thought that I'd go and visit...er...an old school friend. I won't be gone for long." This time he could feel himself blushing deeply: lying to strangers was one thing but to his mother...that was different.

She didn't believe him for a moment. She knew that he had no close friends, so she leapt to the erroneous conclusion that he had met a girl and wanted some privacy. "That's fine, love. Just let me know where you are staying."

"Do you and Karen want anything from the chippy?" he asked, thinking that his ruse had worked.

"No thanks, love. We'll be fine. See you later."

Mike thought for a moment. What had she said? Let her know where I'm staying...he hadn't thought that about accommodation, nor what he needed to take with him. Those thoughts occupied the rest of his evening, following his trip to buy a bag of chips and pocketing the change. He never noticed the shadows that stalked his every move.

***

Jack had arranged to meet Janice at seven-thirty and was planning to take her to a restaurant away from the hotel. He had selected a Chinese establishment next to the covered market in Preston city centre, made the booking, and was about to head for the shower when there was a knock on the door.

"Who is it?" he snapped, frustrated by the interruption to his plan for the evening.

"Rimmer, it's me." Cedric Morgan's voice sounded frail through the door. "Can I speak to you for a moment? I feel that it is somewhat of the essence."

Intrigue got the better of Jack's annoyance at being disturbed. He opened the door and beckoned Morgan inside.

"I've got an appointment this evening, and I need to get ready." Jack said, gesturing towards the only chair in the room.

"With my daughter, perchance?" replied Morgan, although his voice betrayed no emotion at the prospect. "No matter. I must explain something to you." He sat heavily in the only chair.

Taking Jack's silence as permission to continue, he went on.

"I spent my working life in the service of my country, protecting her from the enemy within. I started in nineteen thirty-five, straight from a classics degree at Oxford. At the time, our efforts were concentrated on the Germans. We knew that there was a war coming: it was obvious to everybody except the politicians. But something else had come to my attention. A friend from university had been recruited by MI6, who handled all the foreign stuff. It was against the rules, but we had both been concerned by the number of Communist sympathisers at Oxford. You will remember the famous debate about King and Country in 1933, well, we were there. We were disgusted by the outcome of the debate, of course, but we considered the Communist students to be harmless, and Communism itself to be a passing phase limited to Russia."

Jack listened with growing interest. That debate was something of an historical watershed, but here he was, talking to somebody that had actually been there. Morgan continued.

"Anyway, in the mid-thirties there were rumours circulating about wholesale mass murder in Russia and the other Soviet states. Officially, these rumours remained just that, with Leftist sympathisers denying that anything of the sort was going on in the Workers' Paradise. Then MI6 started to get reports from inside Russia. It turned out that the rumours were true: Stalin was butchering people by the thousand. My friend showed me the reports. They made horrifying reading, Rimmer. It was a Great Terror indeed.

"Anyway, along came the war, starting with the invasion of Poland by both the Germans and the Soviets. Ribbentrop and Molotov's non-aggression pact had taken everybody by surprise: the received wisdom was that the Nazis and the Communists were natural enemies. It made me realise that the Soviets were not above anything to further their aim of world domination. I came to the conclusion that they must be as much our enemy as the Germans, and that they probably had far more sympathisers and agents on our soil. Fortunately, German agents were largely fairly inept and we picked them up quite frequently. That gave me time to concentrate on Communists. In those days, they had comprehensively infiltrated the unions, so all I had to do was to read newspaper reports of strikes or other industrial unrest, and I had my suspects.

"After the war, the Soviets became our official enemies for forty-five years. Let me ask you, Rimmer: who won the Cold War?" Before Jack could answer, Morgan went on.

"The Cold War was supposed to be an ideological conflict between Capitalism and Communism, wasn't it? The collapse of the Soviet Union meant that Capitalism had won, didn't it? Well, I beg to differ. Ever heard of Cultural Marxism, Rimmer? It was thought up by an Italian, Antonio Gramsci. He was a Communist too, and he realised that relatively stable societies, like ours, were never going to see a revolution like that in Russia in 1917. He surmised that the only way to spread Communism was by stealth, by infiltrating the institutions of a country and then causing social breakdown. Do you know what? They have succeeded. The Left now control so much of our public life, from education to the judiciary and local government. Did you know that children never learn about the Great Terror? They are taught about Apartheid and slavery and the Holocaust. That is all right and proper, but they never get to hear about Mao's Cultural Revolution or Pol Pot's Year Zero.

"Just look at the output of the BBC. It is so 'politically correct' it gives a warped view of life. Warped to the Left, of course. Do you know what political correctness is, Rimmer? It's just a part of Cultural Marxism, that's what. All those years of conflict, all my years in the service of my country against Communism were for nothing! They never came through the Fulda Gap in their T72 tanks, Rimmer, because they didn't need to. Their fellow travellers were here all along, destroying our society from the inside."

Morgan, who had been leaning further and further forward as he spoke, collapsed back into the chair. Flecks of spittle spread from the corners of his mouth and his cheeks were flushed. By now, Jack was wondering where this lecture was leading, eager for the dénouement so that he could get ready to go out.

"I needed to tell you this, Rimmer; to get it off my chest. There's more to come, but that can wait until tomorrow. I'm not long for this world, you see, a matter of a few months at the most. But I have to make my peace, don't you see?"

Jack didn't see, but as the old man rose from the chair and headed for the door he was secretly pleased that the homily appeared to have ended. Remembering Morgan's reason for talking to him, Jack felt slightly ashamed at his impatience. The thought of Janice, however, soon overcame his guilt and he headed for the tiny en-suite bathroom.

***

"Are you sure that you're all right?" Steve Melling's concern for his wife was clear from the tone of his voice. They were in the living room of their flat: Katie sat on the settee with her legs curled under her and Steve standing with his back to the window. Joshua had been put to bed, but they could still hear him burbling to himself in his cot.

"Yes. I think that it was a false alarm. It's been a couple of hours now, and nothing's happened. I'm fine, really." The tremor in Katie's voice belied her confidence, although she wasn't sure what had scared her the most: the apparitions or the fear that she was going into premature labour.

"Steve," she continued, "something bad is going to happen. I can feel it. Those other ghosts, they're after somebody and they think that I can bring him here."

"Who? Who do we know that might have had anything to do with... wait a minute. Could this be something to do with old George? Is he the one?" Steve's face took on a determined expression as he recalled the conversation with Jack Rimmer the previous afternoon. "If George derailed a munitions train, maybe there was something else that happened because the train didn't arrive. Jack Rimmer's got a copy of the report: I'll ask him. Where's his mobile number?"

Katie gestured towards the small telephone table that occupied the corner next to the other chair. Steve took the two steps needed to reach the phone and located the number on the pad. Lifting the handset, he dialled the number and waited, his back to Katie. After a moment, the call connected.

"Mr Rimmer, it's Steve Melling. Can I ask you a question?"

Katie couldn't make out what was being said at the other end, but the voice sounded less than happy.

"Sorry to disturb you, but it's just a quick one. You said that you had seen a report from the war about the train being derailed. Can you tell me, was there something else that happened?"

116

The disembodied voice spoke for a minute or so.

"Thank you Mr Rimmer. Sorry again. 'Bye."

Steve turned to Katie, but said nothing for a few seconds. He seemed to be struggling to find the words, but finally he spoke.

"According to the report, the ship that the train was delivering to was delayed in Preston Dock long enough to miss their convoy. They sailed anyway, heading for Alexandria. They never made it: the ship was torpedoed and lost with all hands." Steve's voice began to break and his eyes filled with tears. "Jesus, Katie! I've been drinking with that bloke for over a year, and now he's brought all this on us!" Steve was almost shouting now, desperation creeping into his voice.

In a quieter tone he added: "I've brought all this on us. First the flat, then George. It's all my fault."

Katie stood, wrapped her arms around him and placed her head on his shoulder.

"No it isn't, love. We're in this together, and we'll see it through together. Something tells me that it'll all be over soon, anyway."

***

Despite the interruptions, Jack was in the hotel's reception area at seven twenty-five. Wearing his least-creased trousers and shirt, he paced nervously under the disinterested gaze of the receptionist. During his time at Sandhurst, his etiquette training had told him to be five minutes early for a business appointment and ten minutes late for a social engagement. Jack, however, wasn't taking any chances: he didn't want to run any risk of Janice arriving in reception without him waiting. The ten minutes before Janice appeared seemed interminable but at last she was in front of him, a slightly nervous smile on her face but her eyes bright with anticipation.

Prior to changing, she had spoken briefly with her father. Despite appearing somewhat preoccupied, is demeanour was almost back to normal. He had put his earlier histrionics down to being tired from the journey, and told her that he would have an early night and speak with her the following day. She wasn't entirely convinced, but the prospect of an evening with Jack had overcome her residual concern.

Before leaving home, Janice had spent some considerable time choosing an outfit for this eventuality. She had taken everything out of her wardrobe and laid them out on her bed, fussing over this outfit or that. After about an hour, she had settled on a simple but elegant calf-length pale blue dress, high-necked but sleeveless. A matching pair of low-heeled shoes and a simple gold bangle and pearl drop earrings had completed the ensemble. In her hotel room, she had carefully unpacked the dress, examining it for any creases. Her makeup was understated, and the finishing touch was a dab of Chanel No 5.

To Jack, she had glided gracefully towards him while he stood, butterflies in his stomach like a youth on his first date.

"Ready?" she said, smiling and taking his arm. "Where are you taking me?"

"I hope you like Chinese. I found a restaurant in the city centre" he replied.

"I love Chinese."

Jack led her outside to his car, wishing that he had had the foresight to change the Micra for something a little grander. Ever the gentleman, he opened the passenger door for Janice before walking briskly round to the driver's side and climbing in. Hoping that he had memorised the directions properly, he took the car out of the hotel car park and on to the main road into the city. Fortunately, his nervousness failed to get the better of his memory, and he was glad that he had asked the restaurant for advice where to park. They had informed him that the covered market doubled as a car park in the evening and that he would therefore be able to leave the car right outside.

The sun had set before they had left the hotel, and the night was made darker still by the steadily lowering clouds. As Jack leapt out of the car to open Janice's door once more, the rising wind made his shirt flap about his torso and made him wish that he had brought a jacket, if only to place it around his companion's shoulders.

The meal itself seemed to pass in a blur. Jack joined Janice in a single glass of wine as an aperitif, sticking to water thereafter as Janice sipped her Sauvignon. The food was excellent: the main dishes being served on sizzling platters placed in front of them. The conversation flowed more easily for Jack now that some of his earlier anxiety had dissipated. They talked about their past lives, how they passed the time and their hopes for the future. Neither mentioned the other as part of that future, although both were hoping that it would be the case.

All too soon the meal was at an end, the bill paid and they returned to the car in the strengthening wind. The journey back to the hotel was in silence, each of them wondering what to say, or do next. Jack walked Janice back to her room, his nerves returning in spades. For her part, Janice was determined not to spoil what for her had been a wonderful evening. When they reached her door, she turned to face Jack. Looking him straight in the eye, she regretted, just for an instant, not investing in some lingerie for this occasion. Realising that she wasn't yet ready for the next step, she settle for kissing Jack lightly on the cheek. Stepping back from him momentarily, she moved forward once more and kissed him again, this time fully on the lips. She lingered for just a second, then broke away. Placing her hand on his cheek, she smiled sweetly, bade him goodnight, then turned and entered her room.

Jack, utterly speechless and unable to suppress a grin, returned to his room. Placing the plastic card in its slot under the door handle, he felt as though he was walking on air.

Thursday 0700

Mike Simpson had never known that there was more than one five o'clock each day, but that was the time that his alarm clock rudely interrupted a fantastic dream featuring Emily from the railway museum, a fast car and, bizarrely, Cadbury's Creme Eggs. He had set the clock for that time to ensure that he would be able to shower, dress, pack his overnight bag and make it to the station by seven o'clock. These tasks complete, he had tiptoed down the stairs, raided the fridge for a pork pie and sneaked out of the house past the open door of the lounge where Karen was sleeping on the sofa.

As it was, he had underestimated the length of time that it would take to reach the station: he was rescued by a passing taxi who took him the last three-quarters of a mile to York station. Train travel being new to Mike, he had no idea where to go next. He passed through the entrance hall, into the station proper and immediately saw the information boards on his left. Scanning the destinations, he panicked momentarily when he couldn't find a train to Preston. Fortunately, a member of the station staff was on hand to direct him first to the ticket office (which he had walked past) and then to platform 6 where the train to Blackpool was already waiting.

As he crossed the footbridge over the tracks, Mike remembered that he still didn't know what to do when he got to his destination. He had the maps in his pocket; beyond them he would have to play things by ear. Once again, he didn't notice the shadow that matched his every move. Entering the train, Mike was surprised at the number of people already on board and had to walk to the front of the second carriage of the three-car, maroon coloured train before he found a double seat to himself. The seat itself was broken, the squab having detached from the seat back. Moving further forward, Mike found another pair of seats, threw his backpack on to the luggage rack, and sat next to the grimy window. At this point he discovered the lack of legroom in these trains, and grimaced at the thought of over two hours spent with his knees jammed against the seat in front.

At six minutes past seven, on time, the engines under the front and rear carriages roared and the train slowly departed York station and headed south on the main line. Gazing out of the window, Mike looked up to see that a fine rain was falling from the lowering sky, turning the dirt on the window into an opaque mud and further obscuring his vision. Above the rumble of the diesel engine, he could hear the increasing wind buffeting the train. Forty five minutes and seven stops later, the train had reached Leeds and was completely full, with passengers standing in the aisles and in the door vestibules. Despite the noise and the rising temperature, Mike was fast asleep.

***

When Jack awoke he was still smiling. Sleep had been a long time coming the previous night, but when he had finally succumbed his slumber had been deep and dreamless. The memory of his time with Janice stirred an emotion that he had not felt for many years, if at all. Could she be the one? He certainly hoped so: perhaps he wasn't destined to spend the rest of his life alone after all. Something, however, was lurking at the back of his mind, stalking his consciousness like the suppressed memory that it was. Suddenly, the thought burst to the forefront of his mind: his father's ghost. He hadn't dare raise the subject with Janice, afraid to risk spoiling the simple pleasure of her company by recounting a tale that even he thought too fantastic to believe.

But the subject was still there, and had to be faced. Today. Jack switched on the light, climbed out of bed, made himself a cup of coffee and sat on the edge of the bed to think. As far as his reason for being in Preston was concerned, he really didn't know what to do next. According to the Mellings, the visitations had been becoming more frequent, as if building up to something. And then there was Cedric Morgan's insistence on coming to see him, here of all places. He knew about the Sciron file, but that was the only link, wasn't it?

Another thought occurred to Jack. Steve Melling had asked him about the consequences of the derailment but, in his haste to be with Janice, he had not thought to ask why Steve wanted to know. Had there been another appearance of the ghost? Jack decided that he would speak to Morgan first, then pay a visit to the Mellings.

That left Janice, the person that he wanted to see more than any other. As the thought of her kiss once again pushed all other thoughts aside, Jack heard the howling of the wind outside. Frowning, he went over to the window and peered through a gap in the curtains. Outside, the dawn had been cloaked by the heavy, dark grey clouds that heralded the arrival of the first of the fronts associated with the depression that was generating the gale. Rain lashed down, whipped to an angle by the wind, causing the cars on the road alongside the hotel to throw up sheets of spray that their full-speed wipers struggled to clear. Grimacing, Jack closed the curtains and headed to the bathroom for a shave and a shower.

His ablutions complete, Jack dressed, wishing that he had packed more clothes since he was clearly going to get wet today. Pulling on his coat, he headed to the restaurant to get some breakfast, realising that his first soaking of the day would be between the hotel and the pub where the food was served. As he crossed the hotel lobby, he saw the guest in front of him foolishly trying to keep dry using a collapsible umbrella. The umbrella lived up to its name, collapsing inside-out the instant that the wind hit it and exposing the poor, coatless man to the full force of the downpour. Jack spotted a discarded newspaper. Picking it up, he held it over his head with one hand while the other clasped the lapels of his coat. Thus prepared, Jack ran for his breakfast.

Something's happening, thought Katie Melling as she prepared breakfast for Joshua. The previous day's events, culminating in the false alarm, had left her feeling unsettled. Sleep had been a long time coming: the arms of Morpheus being kept away either by the images crowding her mind, the restlessness of her unborn child or Steve's incessant snoring. Standing in the tiny kitchen, mashing a Weetabix into warm milk, her eyes stared straight ahead and she struggled to concentrate on anything for more than a few moments. But still the same thought kept returning: something is going to happen.

As to the nature of that something, there was no sign. The harbingers of her spectral visitors were all absent: no feelings of sadness, rage or loathing. Her baby was still for once. Outside, the wind howled, the trees on the embankment opposite the flat whipped into a frenzy of swaying branches whilst the rain drummed on the windows. But still her intuition told her that the events of the past ten days were somehow approaching their zenith.

Her thoughts were interrupted by a tug at her dressing gown.

"Want bekfast, Mummy," burbled Joshua, his eyes wide and pleading. Katie looked at him and forced herself to smile.

"Okay, little man," she replied, taking a clean bib from the drawer next to the cooker and fastening it around her son's neck. She then led him by the hand, his breakfast dish in the other, back to the living room where their small dining table was tucked into a corner. Too weary to lift him up, Katie let Joshua climb on to the chair and settle himself down.

Realising that she had forgotten a spoon, Katie put the dish down in front of Joshua and went back into the kitchen. On her return, the little boy had started without her, dipping his hand into the dish then proceeding to spread most of the contents of his hand around his mouth and the surrounding area. He was delving into the glutinous mess for a second go when Katie got to him, snatching hold of his hand. Joshua looked at her in surprise, his face appearing to have a growth of cereal-coloured beard. Katie's nascent anger disappeared immediately; this time her smile was genuine.

At that moment, Steve made a fortuitous entry to the living room, having finished in the bathroom. One glance was sufficient to send him scuttling into the kitchen for cleaning materials. A few minutes later, their son was happily tucking into the remains of his breakfast under the watchful supervision of his father while Katie went to get dressed. On her return, Steve noticed the pensive look on his wife's face.

"Penny for them," he asked.

"It's today," she replied. "I don't know what, exactly, but I have a strong feeling that something is going to happen."

Steve looked out of the window. "There'll be nothing happening at work today," he said. "I'll just ring in, but I think that I need to take the day off."

Katie's reply was distant; virtually whispered. "Somehow, I don't think that I'll make it in today, either."

***

It was a sudden gust of wind driving the rain against the window that woke Janice. Having been woken from a deep sleep, she was momentarily confused by the unfamiliar surroundings. Sitting bolt upright in the bed, she spotted the hotel literature on the desk opposite her which served to remind her of where she was. With the realisation came the memory of the night before, accompanied by a contented smile. She sat for a moment, savouring the recollection of the look of sheer joy on Jack's face as she had closed her bedroom door having kissed him. She was sure of it now: he was the one. But what should her next move be? It was at this point that she recalled just why she was in Lancashire at all, and wondered just what it was that her father had to do so far from home. He had spoken the previous afternoon of being a disappointment to her, but she had no idea quite what he meant by that. The memory of him sitting in her car, tears rolling down his face, suddenly came to the fore, swiftly accompanied by a deep concern for his state of mind.

She decided to ponder the subject as she showered and dressed. Coming out of the small but functional bathroom wrapped in a towel, she parted the curtains slightly to look at the weather. Seeing the driving rain, she opted for the jeans that she had driven in and a simple white blouse. Looking at her reflection in the mirror as she dried her hair, Janice decided that, having sorted things out with her father, she would seduce Jack, that very night. She was convinced that he was too much of a gentleman to make the first move so it would fall to her to lead him on. She began to plot how the evening would go: another restaurant, then back to the hotel...but not this one. Functional as it was, Janice thought that it was unsuitable for the first physical embodiment of true love. No, this was the sort of place people came to for illicit sex. A trip into the city centre was called for, firstly to find somewhere to eat, then a suitably high-class place to stay. There must be somewhere, she reasoned, near Preston that she could get a room for tonight. Cost wasn't really an issue: her late husband had left her well provided for and an occasional extravagance such as this was well within her means. Finally, some appropriate nightwear. A silk nightdress, not too short, in black. No, red. She briefly toyed with the idea of finding a branch of Ann Summers but dismissed it almost as quickly, for now at least.

Realising that they were unsuitable for the day's dreadful weather, she shunned the suede boots from the previous day and pulled from her suitcase a pair of black leather boots with a short but pointed heel. Having pulled them on and tucked her jeans into them, she straightened up and looked once more in the mirror. She paused for a moment, then, thinking that Jack might be at breakfast, undid the top two buttons of her blouse before grabbing her coat and heading for the restaurant.

Thursday 0900

The rain hadn't woken Cedric Morgan: he had lain awake for much of the night. He slept little at his age, his inability to rest not helped by the increasing discomfort from the prostate cancer that was spreading tumours around his body. But it was his guilty conscience that did most to prevent his slumber. Once again, as he had found himself staring at the ceiling in the small hours, he had weighed his lengthy and unblemished service to the nation against his one terrible failure. Once again, he remembered how he was one of the few in MI5 not tainted by the Philby and Burgess affairs. His career had been one of moderate, small scale successes, the only instance that had ever made the papers had been the Profumo case, and he had only been a peripheral participant even then. He often thought about John Profumo, a man of honour in Cedric's opinion who had resigned not only his office but his seat in Parliament and devoted the rest of his life to charity work in the East End of London. Yes, he thought, a man of honour. Not like today's crop of professional politicians; caught sharing a prostitute with a foreign agent they would refuse to admit any wrongdoing and blame the whole affair on the media. A snort of derision had passed his lips at the thought.

But what had it all been for? The Cold War was won, Communism defeated and with it the common enemy that had given purpose to the military and the security services. On top of that, the Communists hadn't been beaten at all: they had simply gone deep underground, infiltrating the national institutions and biding their time until the breakdown of British society ushered in their precious revolution. Had his life's work been in vain? Had the sacrifice of those men not been justified after all?

Morgan knew that today he would have to admit everything.

Janice, his only child, must know the truth, but the person that would understand would be Rimmer. Cedric had noticed the looks exchanged between the two of them, had known that they had dined together the previous evening. She could do worse, he supposed, and Rimmer seemed like a decent sort. He would tell them together, get the shame over in one go. Then he would have to admit to his daughter what he had told Rimmer in their last conversation: the fact that his doctors gave him just a few weeks to live.

His mind made up, he looked at the clock on the television, surprised that it was, for him, so late. Making his way unsteadily into the bathroom, he unpacked his shaving equipment and worked up a rich lather on his face. His razor, a heavyweight safety razor that had served him for more than fifty years, shook gently in his trembling hand. His eyes focussed on themselves in the mirror rather than on his face. By the time he had finished shaving his face sported a collection of tiny rivulets of blood, stemmed by small pieces of tissue. Morgan then washed his face in water as hot as he could bear to remove the blood and close up the cuts, went back into the bedroom and dressed. Despite his efforts, one of the cuts continued to bleed, leaving a dark stain on his shirt collar.

Morgan, despite being habitually fastidious, hadn't noticed. He pulled on his old woollen overcoat, placed a flat cap on his head, and left the room to find his daughter.

***

Janice was, at that moment, standing in the hotel's reception area. She had met a windswept and decidedly damp Jack Rimmer on his return from breakfast. On spotting her heading towards him, Jack's face had broken into the wide grin that was rapidly becoming a permanent feature.

"Morning, Jack," said Janice, her voice just a little more sultry than usual. "Did you sleep well?"

"Like a baby, thank you," Jack replied, immediately conscious that having never had children, he was hardly in a position to use that particular phrase. "You?"

"Yes, despite the rather hard bed. That reminds me; Father never actually said how long we would be here. Do you know?"

As she spoke, Jack was having difficulty concentrating on her words. As a defence against the strong winds, Janice had tied her hair up, exposing the full length of her graceful neck. He was admiring the shape, following its line down, his eye drawn by the open blouse that exposed just a hint of rounded breast. At that instant, Jack could think of nothing he would rather do than to kiss that particular soft, white flesh.

"Jack?" There was a knowing lilt to her voice as she brought him back to the present. His face flushed red, his embarrassment exacerbated by the slight smile on Janice's lips.

"Sorry," he grinned, sheepishly. "I spoke to your father last night, but he gave no hint as to what you are doing here. He just kept talking about, well, things. Kept on about how the Communists had won after all, or something. He wasn't making much sense, to be honest."

Jack didn't mention that following the mention of the Oxford Union debate, he hadn't really been listening until Morgan's announcement of his impending demise. He wondered for a second whether Janice knew about the state of her father's health, but decided immediately that it wasn't his place to tell her. Not yet, anyway.

"I have some people to see this morning regarding the story that I am working on, but I can't see me needing to be here much longer."

"Is that the story that you interviewed Father about last Sunday? Is it interesting?"

"Well, quite possibly, yes. At least, from a personal point of view it is. I have been looking into the disappearance of my father and some...er...fresh evidence has come to light."

He didn't dare mention the ghostly element to all of this: he barely believed it himself and he had no doubt that his nascent relationship with Janice would be put at risk if her dared admit to her what he had been told, and what he increasingly had no option but to believe.

"I have two more visits to make, and..." his voice trailed off as another thought occurred to him. How did Steve Melling know about the ship? His father's ghost couldn't have told him: he had died before the ship had departed Preston Docks. Another piece to the puzzle that Jack would have to make fit.

"And what?" Once again, Janice's voice brought his attention back to where it should be.

"Er...and then perhaps we can spend some more time together?" Nice one, thought Jack.

"I'd be delighted," replied Janice. "Maybe we'll make it to breakfast together tomorrow morning."

Winking suggestively, she kissed Jack lightly on the cheek, pulled her coat around herself and headed out to the restaurant.

***

Mike Simpson felt a hand shaking his shoulder which stirred him from his slumber. Groggily opening his eyes, he looked out of the train window to see that they were crossing a metal girder bridge over a river that looked like it was at least fifty feet below the railway. The train manager was announcing their arrival at Preston and Mike turned to the person that had woken him at such an opportune moment. The seat next to him was empty, and it occurred to him that he hadn't told anybody where he was getting off. His ticket hadn't been checked; the train had been packed for most of the journey making it impossible for anybody to make a meaningful attempt to check travel documents between the frequent stops. Must have dreamt it, he thought.

Unravelling himself from the position in which he had slept for the past two hours, Mike retrieved his bag and joined the throng that was queuing to get to the door as the train pulled into the platform. He couldn't help marvelling that he had actually managed to get this far, and allowed himself a congratulatory grin. As he alighted, the wind, funnelled through the station building, howled and moaned and plucked at Mike's thin top. Rooting in his bag, he extracted a lightweight anorak and pulled it over his head without unzipping it. He then followed the crowd, assuming that they were all heading for the exit. The multitude directed him up some steps, over a bridge spanning the tracks, down another staircase and into the central aisle of the station. At this point, he once again realised that he still didn't know where to go next. Pulling his map from a pocket in his bag, he studied the area that he thought his search for answers should start.

"Lost, are you?" The voice came from a diminutive Asian man dressed in the long grey overcoat issued by Virgin trains to its station staff. "Can I help?"

"Yeah, thanks," replied Mike. "I'm trying to get to this place here."

He pointed to his destination on the map to the man who took it from him and thought for a moment.

"Right. Do you know Preston at all?" When Mike shook his head, the man continued. "You need to go up those steps there," he pointed to another staircase opposite the one Mike had just descended. "Go out of the door, then straight across the road into the shopping centre. Follow your nose, up an escalator then to the front door of the centre. Turn right out of the front, and you will see three bus stops in a row. Go to the furthest one, then catch the one-eleven bus. Ask the driver to drop you off at the Bridge Inn."

Thanking the man, Mike followed his directions out of the station. As he exited the building, the wind and rain almost slammed into him. Pulling the hood of his coat up, Mike ran over the zebra crossing between the station and the shopping centre, only to wait for what seemed like ages as the automatic door opened in front of him. Inside the centre, he walked towards the escalator that he could see at right angles ahead of him. Taking it up one floor, he was momentarily confused as all he could see ahead was the entrance to Debenham's coffee shop. Realising that people were approaching from his left, Mike turned that way and, after a few yards, spotted the exit to the shopping centre. Passing through another automatic door, the entrance extended beyond the door giving some shelter as Mike looked for the bus stop. Spying the row of steel and glass shelters, he made a dash for the first one, waited for a moment, then sprinted once more past the second to the last one.

He didn't have long to wait before a green single-deck bus, sporting the appropriate number, approached down the bus lane that took up half the street. Five minutes later, having made the appropriate request of the driver, Mike found himself once more out in the full force of the terrible weather. The bus stop was placed next to a large stone wall, with a matching edifice on the opposite side of the road. It only took Mike a moment to realise that he was looking at a pair of bridge abutments. The one opposite had tall, mature trees on top which were waving wildly as they were buffeted by the gale. An embankment curved away to the left, behind the houses on the other side. Mike crossed the road quickly, seeking shelter as well as being drawn towards what he recognised from the map as the remains of Ribble Junction. Following the path at the foot of the embankment, the same place where, although Mike couldn't know it, George Williams had been spooked two days earlier. The embankment was lined by a wooden fence which was broken down in places and Mike used one of the gaps to clamber up onto the muddy slope and climb to the level area at the top.

Inside the canopy of the trees, the wind was less violent and the rain fell a little more vertically. Mikes jeans were already wet through and clung to his legs as he made his way away from the road. Ahead of him, the former track bed went either straight away from the road or, as he had observed before, headed off to the left. Choosing the straight route, Mike walked for no more than a hundred yards before being brought to a halt by a thin wire fence stretched across in front of him. Wiping the rain from his eyes, Mike could see that there was a gap in the embankment ahead where a path had once been bridged by the railway. Turning back, he took the alternative path. The trees seemed closer together this way, forming a dense wood that prevented him walking in a straight line for more than a couple of paces. Rounding one particularly large tree, Mike suddenly came face to face with a man who, like himself, was dripping wet.

Overcoming his initial shock, Mike realised that the man was standing still, just staring at him. Furthermore, he wasn't wearing a coat, just some brown overalls and what looked like a life jacket. At that moment, the stench of rotting seaweed struck Mike's nostrils, like the smell that had heralded the appearance of the spectres at home but much, much stronger. He suddenly felt the presence of more people, crowding round him, but couldn't see anybody else. Panicking, he turned to run, but his legs had turned to jelly. The smell, the feelings of hatred that he had experienced before, combined and grew stronger, blotting out all normal sensations. Mike felt himself falling, losing consciousness. Just before everything went black, he heard a voice hiss in his ear.

Now you will help us.

Thursday 1000

The wind found every gap in the wooden sash windows on the front of George Williams' house, generating a cacophony of moaning and rattling. Rain was seeping in too, making George even angrier than his normally cantankerous disposition. To make matters worse, the paper boy had left his newspaper stuck halfway out of the letterbox and when George had finally made his way downstairs to retrieve it the paper had simply fallen apart; the half in his hand having detached from the grey lump of papier maché that constituted the portion that was exposed to the elements.

The nearest newsagent was just over the bridge on the other side of the river. It was a ten minute walk in normal conditions, but there was no way that George would walk very far in the storm. Instead, he rummaged through the scraps of paper next to the telephone that constituted his address book, finally finding Kevin Anderson's mobile number. Furiously stabbing at the buttons on the telephone, his mood was not improved when, in his haste, he dialled a wrong number. Slamming the handset back on to the body of the device, he closed his eyes and took a deep breath to calm himself before making another attempt. This time the number was correct, although it rang for a considerable time before a sleepy voice answered it.

"Kevin, George here. Can you come round?" George told Kevin about his newspaper, exaggerating the importance of his need to have a copy by claiming that there was a big railway story in that day's edition.

"Er...yeah...hang on a minute." George could hear Kevin talking to his mother, with whom he now lived again, asking if he could borrow her car. Clearly, he hadn't told her about his driving ban, as she agreed without hesitation.

"Be there in ten minutes," said Kevin. "Bye." George didn't bother replying.

Twenty minutes later, a car horn sounded outside. George peered through the bay window but could see nothing. Deciding that it must be Kevin, he pulled on the old woollen railway coat that had served him for nearly forty years and dashed outside, pausing only to slam the front door behind him. By the time that he reached the car, George's legs below the calf-length coat were soaked and rain had forced its way past his collar and was running down his neck. Inside the car the environment was little better; it may have been dry but Kevin was in need of a bath and some clean clothes. The smell of body odour was so strong George almost gagged. Without a word, he imperiously waved his hand to indicate that Kevin should drive on.

Ten minutes later, the route in a car being somewhat longer than on foot, they were parked outside the newsagent. George scuttled inside, reappearing a few minutes later with his hand inside his coat. Kevin turned the car around and set off back towards George's house. The route to the shop had taken them past the stone abutments adjacent to the Bridge Inn, and as the car approached them once more a long-haired young man, dressed in jeans and an anorak, stepped into the road, turning to stare at the occupants.

Kevin, swearing loudly, reacted quickly enough to stop the car ten feet from the youth, who didn't flinch. Opening the door, Kevin began to remonstrate with the lad, every other word beginning with 'f'. The youth simply ignored him, continuing to stare at the car. George watched between sweeps of the windscreen wipers as Kevin approached the young man, noting with some discomfort that he was the target of the strangely lifeless eyes. Kevin had got within a yard of the dripping figure when the acne-scarred face head suddenly turned to stare at him instead. At the same time, Kevin suddenly felt the malice in the eyes that fixed upon him. There was something about this man, something that made the normally fearless (when it came to fists) Kevin Anderson stop in his tracks. For probably the first time, Kevin was truly afraid, but he didn't know why. Avoiding eye contact, he slowly backed away. The youth's head turned back to the car, and George felt as though the eyes were burning into him.

The young man lifted his right arm and extended his index finger, pointing at George.

Come with us.

It was those voices again, the same ones that had terrified George on the pathway only a few yards from where he now sat. Frozen in his seat, George could do nothing as the youth approached his side of the car and opened the door. Again, he heard the voices:

Come with us.

George realised at that moment that the lad's lips weren't moving, although it seemed as though the sounds emanated from him. Fixated by the staring eyes, George felt utterly compelled to obey the command. The youth turned and began to walk away. Kevin could only stand and watch, helpless, as his mentor followed the silent figure past the abutments and down the path next to the Methodist Church. As they rounded the corner, Kevin felt as if a weight had been taken from his shoulders. Pausing for long enough to close the car door, he ran towards where they had disappeared. Turning the corner, his eyes frantically searched for any sign of either man. The wind tugged at his sodden track suit and the rain streamed down his face as he realised that both had simply vanished.

***

"Shall we return to the scene of the crime?" Even more subdued than the previous evening, Cedric Morgan's voice had an air of resignation. "Presumably you were wondering why I wanted to meet you here." This was clearly a statement, not a question.

Jack had no intention of disputing the point.

"You mean the old railway, don't you." Another statement.

"Yes, yes I do. Despite the weather, I feel that it would be...ah... appropriate. Let's find my daughter and get this over with."

Telling Morgan to meet him in reception, Jack made his way to Janice's room. Glad of an excuse to speak to her again, he was disappointed when there was no answer to his knocking. Jack knew that she had been heading for the restaurant an hour before; he also knew that the surroundings in there were not conducive to lingering over breakfast. Not alone, anyway. Suppressing the slight but irrational frustration generated by her absence, Jack tried ringing her mobile number. The call went straight to voicemail.

"Er...hi...er...Janice, it's...er...Jack," he had always felt stupid talking to machines, and this occasion was no exception. "Can you...er... give me a call when you get this. Love you." Jack had thumbed the red button on his handset before realising what he had just said. Ah, well, he thought, it's said now. Two minutes later, when he rejoined Morgan, he was still smiling.

Cedric, however, was not amused. "I specifically wanted to talk to you both together," he snapped, angrily. "I know about you and her, Rimmer, don't deny it. She'll need somebody, and she could do worse than you."

"Thanks," muttered Jack, not knowing whether he was being flattered or insulted. Was it that obvious? Morgan was right, though, despite his advanced years, the news of his medical condition would still be a shock to his daughter.

"Well, let's get on with it. I'll just have to talk to her later," continued Morgan, ignoring Jack's reply. "Will you take me there or not?"

"As it happens, I was going that way. I'd like you to meet some people that I was going to talk to this morning. At least their flat will be more comfortable than my car. Wait here, I'll bring the car round."

Ten minutes after departing the hotel car park, with the Micra's wipers at full speed barely clearing the windscreen and the little car being buffeted by the gusts, Jack's mobile rang. Pulling over into the forecourt of a second-hand car dealership, Jack pulled the handset from his coat pocket and pressed the green button.

"Jack Rimmer," he said.

"I love you too" came the reply.

"Janice! Where are you?" Jack's heart had soared at her words, while her father sat and scowled next to him.

"I needed to do some shopping, so I headed into town. I got lost a couple of times, which is why it took so long for me to call you back. So, apart from declarations of love, was there another reason for your call?"

Jack was speechless for a moment. Gathering his wits, he remembered the real reason why he had called in the first place and explained quickly.

"He was acting strangely yesterday, but last time I spoke to him he was back to his usual grumpy self. Whatever he wants to say, I'd say that he'll have to wait. You two get on with your man talk, and I'll see you both later." She paused for a second. "I meant it, Jack. I really do love you."

Before he could answer, she had hung up. They resumed the journey, Jack struggling to concentrate in the foul conditions. It took them a full ten minutes to cover the last two miles, but eventually Jack was able to park the car in the lee of the stone abutment opposite the Mellings' flat.

***

There was a knock at the door, causing Steve and Katie to look at each other quizzically.

"Are we expecting anybody?" asked Steve.

Katie shrugged. "Not as far as I know."

Steve made his way to the door and looked through the peep hole. The elderly man at the door was a stranger to him. Opening the door, Steve peered around it. Spotting Jack Rimmer standing behind the windswept and decidedly soggy stranger, he pulled the door fully open.

"Morning, Jack. For some reason, I'm not surprised to see you this morning. Who's your friend?"

"Hello, Steve. This is the gentleman that I told you about; the one that wrote the report. His name is Cedric Morgan, and he has come to tell us exactly what happened."

Steve stepped to one side, waving the men inside. "You'd better come in, then. Shall I put the kettle on?"

"Thank you, yes," replied Jack. "Cedric, this is Steve Melling. He and his wife Katie would like to hear what you have to say."

Jack had had some difficulty in persuading Morgan to speak in front of the Mellings, but the din generated by the rain hammering on the roof of Jack's car, even in the relative shelter of the former bridge abutment, had made conversation virtually impossible. The two men had dashed, as much as Morgan could dash anywhere, from the car into the entrance lobby of the flats as another resident had left to battle the elements. Jack had helped the elder man up the two flights of stairs, and both had paused for breath before knocking at the Mellings' door.

Steve took their dripping coats, taking them into the bathroom and draping them over the rail that supported the shower curtain. Jack smiled at Joshua, who waved back, stared blankly at Morgan and returned to the serious business of attacking a colouring book with a crayon.

Katie beckoned the two men to sit. "So, Mr Morgan, can you explain the presence of ghosts in my flat?"

Morgan was shocked by her question. "Ghosts? What nonsense is this?" he snapped.

"It's not nonsense, Cedric," said Jack. "I met this young couple by accident last week. I didn't believe them at first, but they have been able to tell me things that they could not possibly have known without some sort of inside knowledge. So, either this is an elaborate hoax, or they are telling the truth."

"What truth? What are you talking about?" Morgan's voice had an hysterical edge to it. "You never said anything about ghosts."

"Would you have believed me? Of course not. But this family have been experiencing visits by a particular ghost. My father, Cedric."

Morgan paled. His eyes darted around the room, as if searching for the spectre for himself.

When he spoke again, there was steel in Jack Rimmer's voice. "Would you like to tell us the full story now, Cedric?"

The older man seemed to deflate in front of Jack's eyes. His head was bowed and his mouth was moving soundlessly, as if he was rehearsing his next words. When he spoke, his voice was barely a whisper.

"I'm truly sorry, Rimmer. I hope that you can find it in your heart to forgive me."

"Forgive you for what?" It was Katie who spoke.

Cedric Morgan lifted his head, pushed his shoulders back and looked Jack in the eye.

"It was me, Rimmer. I killed him."

Thursday 1100

"Man coming."

It was Joshua who broke the silence following Morgan's admission. Katie Melling could feel it too; once again the atmosphere in the flat was changing as a sense of despondency permeated the people crowded into the small living room. Katie looked at her son, watching for the signs of fear that he had exhibited last time they were visited by the ghost of Jack Rimmer Senior along with "the others". Whoever they were. This time, to her palpable relief, the little boy's concentration never wavered from his artistic endeavours.

"What? Are you expecting somebody else?" Cedric Morgan's eyes flicked from Katie to Jack Rimmer, searching for an explanation.

"He's coming back, isn't he," said Steve, standing in the doorway, the tea forgotten.

"Who? Who is coming back? What are you talking about?" Morgan's voice had a pleading, hysterical edge to it now.

"Jack's father. Or, rather, his ghost," said Katie. "He's been a regular visitor for the past week or so." Her voice was flat, emotionless. Morgan could do nothing but stare at her, confusion and disbelief etched on his face. Jack Rimmer, too, was speechless: the prospect of actually meeting his dead father forcing him to run a gamut of conflicting emotions. He knew that he ought to feel *something* toward Morgan, something more about the death of his father, but it occurred to him that it would be difficult to grieve for somebody that he had never known.

"The past couple of days, there have been others, too," continued

Katie. We haven't really seen them, but they are after somebody. Are you that somebody, Mr Morgan?"

"Did you cause the sinking of the ship, too, Mr Morgan?" added Steve.

Cedric Morgan seemed to have physically shrunk as they spoke. "Yes, I am responsible for that, too," he murmured. "I incited a group of local men, Communist party members, to prevent a munitions train from reaching the docks. They demolished a railway tunnel close to the docks themselves, but there was another way around for the train.

"I followed one of the men to see what they would do next. They met down by the river, then came to this railway to stop the train coming this way. One of them climbed up the telegraph pole next to the track and cut some wires to slow the train down enough that they could unbolt a couple of rails. They had a long spanner for that purpose. When Rimmer appeared, I panicked. I picked up the spanner and swung it at him. I told myself afterwards that I only meant to knock him out, but to be honest I was so determined to discredit the Communists that I really don't know what I was thinking at that moment.

"Anyway, we buried the body in the remains of an old signal box that must have been quite close to here. The train was delayed, but not for too long, and I returned to London thinking that the operation hadn't been a total disaster. A few days later I learned that the ship had missed its convoy but had continued anyway. A U-boat caught up with it, and it was sunk with all hands.

"I wrote up the report to cover my involvement, blaming everything on a fictional spy that I called Sciron. Except that Sciron wasn't fictitious, he was real.

"I was Sciron."

***

George Williams had never felt such a dreadful combination

of being cold, wet and terrified. The youth had dragged him wordlessly up the embankment, hauling on George's coat with every frequent slip. Having reached the top of the bank, there was no pause for breath or respite for George's aching legs. On top of everything else, he was suffering from particularly bad indigestion.

He was led along the line of the former railway alignment, from, as he remembered despite his fear, the old Ribble Junction towards Middleforth Junction. George hadn't walked up here for decades, but in his mind he could see the steam locomotives pulling their loads past his signal box. Tourists heading for Southport, perhaps, or freight bound for the docks at Preston. With his recall of the trains came the memory of Jack Rimmer, triggering a wave of guilt to add to the mixture of feelings.

Suddenly, the youth stopped, and George saw that they had reached the edge of the abutment on Stricklands Lane. Looking ahead, he could see the new estate, not realising that he could look into the living room of his drinking partner Steve Melling.

"What's going on?" asked George, finally gathering enough breath to speak. The youth looked at him, but did not reply. George moved into the partial shelter of a large tree while the youth's blank stare followed his every move. He pulled the collar of his coat up, trying in vain to stem the flow of rainwater down his neck. Having stopped moving, George began to shiver, whether through cold or fear he couldn't tell. He tried repeating the question, but to no avail.

There was a momentary lull in the wind, and the youth stepped away from George. With the howling of the gale through the trees much reduced, George realised that he could hear voices.

"Help! Help me! I'm being mugged!" shouted George as loud as he could, hoping that the voice's owner was in a position to rescue him.

There is nobody to help you.

George looked at the youth again, but his expression hadn't changed. The same blank stare, conveying nothing. Had he spoken? As he searched the boy's face for any signs of emotion, he heard the voice again.

We have come for you, and the other one.

All at once, George was surrounded by figures, moaning, shouting incomprehensibly, but above all looking at him. Some were pointing at him, and they all seemed to crowd closer and closer, blocking his view of the flats and finally shutting out the surrounding trees.

"What do you want with me!" screamed George, utterly terrified.

You killed us. You must atone.

"I never killed anyone! It wasn't me! Please, leave me be." George was sobbing now, his fear exacerbated by the embarrassment that he had wet himself. His indigestion was getting worse, and he felt as though somebody had placed a belt around his chest and was slowly tightening it.

George, listen to me. We did it; we caused these people to die.

"Who...Who's that!" The pain in his chest was getting worse, but there was something familiar about the voice.

George, it's Bill. Young George Peters is here too. It's time for you to join us.

***

"That's odd, he's normally put in an appearance by now." Katie could still feel the intense sadness that heralded the approach of their spectral visitor. Standing with her back to the window, she looked around the room, her eyes taking in the rather pathetic figure of Cedric Morgan sat in the chair and, behind him, Jack Rimmer.

"Perhaps it's you, Jack," she continued. "Maybe he doesn't want to show himself while you're here. Could be he's afraid of seeing his own son as a man older than he was, or he wants to spare you the shock of seeing him like he is now."

Jack, who could sense the changed atmosphere and was feeling distinctly uncomfortable, debated with himself whether he should remain in the flat. After a few moments' thought, he decided that discretion was the better part of valour and that he would test Katie's theory. Muttering a promise to return, he left the flat, made his way down the stairs and made a dash for the car. Sitting in the Micra, the rain drumming on the roof was drowning out the howling of the wind but neither was registering with Jack. His mind was filled with conflicting images of Janice and her father, intermingled with guilt at having left the flat. Jack had looked up to Morgan, respected him and the part that he had played in keeping Britain's enemies at bay. Now, all he could feel was, what? One moment he was merely saddened and disappointed; the next he was positively disgusted. *That man killed my father; yet I am more disappointed at his treachery than the murder of a man I never knew*. So that was his news. That was why he had made his daughter drive all that way, just to ease his guilty conscience. A snort of derision passed Jack's lips; then his emotions swung again. How would he tell Janice? How would she react? Jack was sure of his feelings: the growing malice that he bore Morgan changed nothing about the man's daughter. But would the converse be true? There was only one way to find out. She had to know the truth, and she had to hear it from Jack, face to face. He picked up his mobile phone.

At that moment, Janice was standing in the Ann Summers store that she had spotted as she came out of the front door of Marks and Spencer's. The shop wasn't en route to the car park, but she couldn't resist a peek inside. Once through the door, she felt mildly embarrassed to be in there, wondering what the staff must be thinking about a woman of her age in such a place. Of course, they had seen it all before, men and women of all ages frequented the establishment and one more woman in her sixties was nothing unusual. Janice was wondering if she could get into one particularly revealing garment when her phone rang. Looking at the caller's name on the screen, she put on her sultry voice.

"Jack, do you know where I am right now?"

"What...er...sorry, Janice. I'm afraid we need to meet up. Your father has made a rather...well...an admission. Can we meet back at the hotel? It's important."

The tone in Jack's voice dispelled the disappointment that she felt: whilst her search for a nightdress had been successful, she hadn't yet been able to find alternative accommodation.

"I'll be there, Jack," she said, her voice back to normal. "About twenty minutes?"

Jack agreed, and with that she pulled her coat around herself and stepped once more into the storm.

***

As the M6 bypasses Preston, there are four lanes of traffic in each direction. As the motorway reaches the northern extremity of the city, the north-bound side splits, with lanes one and two curving away to the west to form the M55 to Blackpool, whilst lanes three and four continue northwards towards Lancaster and Carlisle. In the atrocious weather, most drivers had moderated their speed to take into account the visibility that had been vastly reduced by the driving rain and the resultant spray from the tyres of the preceding vehicles. Most, but not all. It was, inevitably, the driver of a high-sided white van who, considering himself God's gift to the internal combustion engine, was paying no heed to the conditions. The climb out of the Ribble valley had slowed him slightly, but as he passed the exit-only junction 31a his speed was back up to eighty-five. Sat in lane four, the driver cursed anybody who dared to obstruct his progress, angrily flashing his headlights from a distance of no more than twenty feet from the rear of the vehicle in front.

The rear of the van was half filled with cleaning supplies; bulky, but not particularly heavy. The driver's next delivery was to a biscuit factory in Blackpool, followed by a suite of offices in Fleetwood. He was late, but that was the fault of the weather, and the "Sunday drivers" that continued to impede his advance. To drown out the noise of the weather, the driver had the CD player turned up as loud as it would go, and, chewing gum, his jaw moved in time to the bass that made the windows rattle.

It was the screen lighting up on his mobile phone that caught his eye. Turning the CD player off, he picked up the handset and answered the call. The caller was his girlfriend, ringing to continue an unfinished argument from the night before. Unwilling to concede any sort of moral victory to the woman, the driver engaged her in the quarrel, having to shout to make himself heard over the din generated by the rain striking the van. He was in mid-rant when he realised that the turn onto the M55 was only a hundred yards away, and he was on the wrong side of the motorway. Without so much as a glance in his nearside mirror, the driver attempted to cut across two lanes. As the van swung left, it leaned to the right. At that moment, a freak gust struck the left hand side of the van, causing it to over-balance. Unable to do anything to prevent a crash, the driver swore and held on to the steering wheel as the van skidded along the tarmac until its energy was expended. The grey underside of the van was virtually invisible to oncoming drivers: the next car had no chance of stopping before colliding with the rear axle. There was sufficient residual energy from that collision to send the van spinning across lane two, where it was struck by another two cars. The innocent victims of the initial crashes were quickly joined by others as cars and lorries, blinded by the spray, piled into the back of each other.

In the van, the cleaning materials had spilled and were now combining to release noxious gases into the interior, removing any chance of survival for the now unconscious driver. By the time vehicles approaching the scene were able to stop, no fewer than forty-six had suffered collisions of varying severity. Those who were uninjured used their mobile phones to summon the emergency services; within six minutes there was a fleet of fire engines and ambulances heading for the carnage.

Thursday 1130

Despite the disappearance of Jack Rimmer, the living room in the Mellings' flat felt crowded. As Jack left the building, the miserable atmosphere heralding the approach of his father's ghost became tangible, intensifying at a faster rate than Katie had felt before. Standing with his back to the window, it was Steve that saw him first; he had been gazing intently at the doorway but occasionally glancing at his wife, who was sitting on the settee. One moment the doorway was empty, the next time that Steve looked up the tall, gaunt figure had appeared. The grey face held an expression of sad determination, the black eyes fixed on Cedric Morgan. Joshua looked up, saw that this visit was different, and went back to his colouring.

You came.

Morgan, who had been holding his head in his hands, sat bolt upright. His head slowly turned towards the voice, a gasp of horror emanating from his lips as he laid eyes on the spectral remains of a man that he had last seen one night more than six decades previously.

"Dear God," was all he could say, his voice barely managing a whisper. It was Katie who spoke next.

"Are the others coming, Jack?" she asked, her fear apparent. The ghost's gaze didn't leave Morgan's face.

They are waiting for you.

"Wh...who is waiting for me? What do you mean?" The old man was plainly terrified now, his eyes bulging as he stared at the visage whose mouth didn't move as the words came out.

The others are waiting. The men that drowned because of you. You must go to them.

"And if I don't go, what then?" Despite his terror, some boldness was asserting itself.

Then they will come for you here.

"No!" screamed Katie. "Don't bring them back here!" Steve moved to her side and placed an arm around her shoulders, staring at Morgan with something approximating hate in his eyes. Joshua began to cry, shocked by his mother's outburst.

Morgan's defiance deflated as abruptly as it had arisen. "Yes, of course," he said, weary resignation in his voice. "Where are they?"

Jack Rimmer's ghost raised his right arm, one bony finger outstretched, pointing across the road to the stone abutment opposite the flat. All eyes followed the direction that was indicated.

"That's George Williams!" said Steve, seeing the old man slumped against a tree. "Who's that with him?"

They could all see the young man standing next to George, staring at them from atop the embankment. As they looked, his arm raised in a beckoning motion. The movement was repeated, just once, then the young man turned and walked back into the trees, quickly disappearing from sight.

"I can't leave old George out there," said Steve. "I'd better go and get him."

No.

"But he's an old man! He'll catch his death out there in this weather!" pleaded Steve.

He must answer for his actions too.

"But he was fooled into it by *him*!" the last word was spat out by Steve as he pointed at Morgan. The spectre didn't answer, so

Steve moved past him into the hall way and grabbed his coat from the hook on the back of the front door. He was about to open the door when he heard Katie scream once more.

"Steve!" His name was followed by a cry of pain. Steve dropped his coat and went back into the living room. Katie was perched on the edge of the settee, her back arched and her legs apart. A small puddle of fluid was gathering at her feet.

"Oh, Steve! It's the baby! My waters have broken!

***

Jack Rimmer had reached the hotel before Janice and was pacing the length of the reception area, rehearsing what he would say to her. The receptionist was watching him, bemused by his silent mouthing of words, usually followed by a frustrated shake of the head. Then the process would begin again. Whatever Jack thought of sounded wrong; either too sharp, too long winded, too trite or just plain silly. He realised that he was going to have to come clean about the supernatural happenings, but that Janice would have to be taken to the Mellings' flat if Jack was not to sound as though he had taken leave of his senses.

The problem was that he wasn't sure that he believed it himself. It was quite a leap of faith to suppress logic and accepted knowledge on the say so of a woman in her twenties. Part of his belief in Katie Melling, and her husband, stemmed from the fact that he *wanted* to believe them, yet his satisfaction at solving the mystery of what happened to his father was tainted by the revelation that his father's murderer was a man who had been something of a hero to Jack. Cedric Morgan had been part of, indeed had created, history. His exploits with MI5 were legendary in certain circles, but all that he had achieved in the service of his country now had to be reassessed in light of his admission. Jack wondered for a moment whether he could write a biography of Morgan, something that the old man had always resisted. Jack had put that down to old school modesty: now he knew the truth. But would Janice let him?

It was as that question framed itself in his mind that Janice walked into the hotel, her carefully arranged hair now plastered to her scalp by the deluge and her coat dripping. Her eyes met his, fixing him with a stare that had reduced the most recalcitrant student to instant submission.

"So, Jack, what's the story?"

"Please, Janice, sit down," said Jack, gesturing towards the low chairs. "Do you want a coffee or something?"

"No, thank you, Jack," she replied. "I've had time to think in the car, and I'm worried about my father. Where is he, by the way?"

"I took him to visit some people that have been, ah, helping me. They are part of the story, and I'll take you to them shortly."

Janice appeared to be satisfied with his answer but her gaze never wavered. Taking a deep breath, Jack continued.

"I've spent the past few minutes trying to come up with a way of telling you this, but I'm going to have to just tell you. Before I do, I want you to know that this changes nothing between us, at least as far as I am concerned."

This seemed to have an unnerving effect on Janice, and she broke off eye contact. Looking away, out of the window to her left, she asked him to tell her.

"I'm really sorry to be the one to tell you, Janice, and I know that your father had intended to tell us together. The thing is," he paused for a moment, still searching for some way to ease the blow. "The thing is, Cedric killed my father, and was responsible for the sinking of a British merchant ship with all hands."

***

As Steve Melling rushed to his wife's side, Cedric Morgan looked again at the ghost of the man that he had killed so many years previously. The spectre held his gaze, but there appeared to be no malice in the dark eyes. Instead, the face conveyed a sense of relief, as though his troubles were finally about to end. The figure turned and walked out of the door, quickly disappearing from sight. Seeing that the Mellings were, not surprisingly, paying him no heed, Morgan pulled himself up out of the chair and moved towards the door.

He knew that his time on Earth was up: perhaps whatever awaited him outside would be preferable to spending the next few weeks being eaten away by the spreading cancer, living his last days in a morphine-induced haze suffering the indignity of being unable to manage the most basic bodily functions for himself. No, he was already resigned to death and it would be better to end it here, now. His only real regret was that his daughter would not be with him, but at least she would be spared the mental anguish of seeing him reduced to a state of utter helplessness.

Letting himself out of the flat, Morgan made his way slowly down the stairs. On reaching the front door, he paused for a moment, straightening his back, pulling back his shoulders, determined to meet his fate with dignity. Pulling the door open, the rain burst through the gap, instantly soaking Morgan's face and hair: he had left his cap in the flat. Walking outside, he carefully closed the door behind him and crossed the road to the former abutment opposite. The end of the stonework nearest him was too high: there was no means of gaining access to the embankment. Moving to the other end, Morgan saw that, just around the corner formed by a lane that paralleled that side of the former railway, there was an easier slope, protected by a wire fence. As he turned the corner, he failed to notice a Nissan Micra turn into Stricklands Lane.

Morgan slipped one leg through the fence, between the top and second strands of wire, then ducked down and squeezed himself through. Attempting to pull the other leg towards himself, he overbalanced and fell on to the grass. Picking himself up, he began to walk up the slope, occasionally being forced to lean so far forward that he fell on to his hands. Persevering, he finally reached the top. The exertion was making him puff hard now; leaning against a tree to regain his breath he was startled by the sight of the youth that had been looking at him through the flat window. Standing just a few feet in front of him, the youth stared at Morgan, giving him the opportunity to study the face in front of him. This one was different: he looked, well, normal. Just that unnerving stare and the lack of verbal communication, not that he could be heard above the howling of the wind; apart from that he looked like any other young man.

The youth turned and walked away, taking the left fork along the old railway alignment. There was nothing familiar about the scene: last time Morgan had been here it had been dark and nature had not reclaimed the land. As they walked, Morgan a few feet behind the young man, he began to sense that they were not alone. A sense of hatred now filled the air, and a hubbub of indistinct voices was accompanied by a strong smell of salt water. As the feeling grew stronger and the voices louder, the youth stopped and turned to face him. Now a fire seemed to blaze in the young man's eyes: suddenly Morgan was surrounded by ghostly figures, all pointing towards him and shouting incoherently. One voice seemed to rise above all the others, although Morgan was unable to determine which figure it came from. Turning from side to side, fear and panic now rising within him, Morgan's eyes finally fell once more on the youth that had led him to this spot. As they did so, that voice spoke again, blotting out not only the cacophony of loathing, but managing to silence the storm itself.

Listen to me

The others died straight away, but not me

I was trapped in the sinking ship, in a pocket of air

It lasted for three days. Three days to think about my wife and child, with no hope of ever seeing them again

You have caused so much suffering

Now you will pay for your crime!

***

Kevin Anderson had returned to his mother's car, angry and confused by what he had witnessed. Noble actions were not a usual part of his personality but, he reasoned, since he was soaking wet anyway, he may as well have another look for George. Returning to the path where they had vanished, Kevin followed it for a short distance. On his left, there was a break in the fence with clear footprints in the mud. On an impulse, he scrambled up the bank, slipping twice and caking his tracksuit bottoms in mud before reaching the top. The footprints had disappeared, and the embankment offered three possible directions. One, he quickly discovered, led back to Leyland Road close to where he had abandoned the car. Of the other two, there was no indication as to where they led or which one George may have taken.

After a moment's indecision, Kevin chose the left-hand path. Pushing his way through the trees, oblivious to the rain that gathered on the leaves to form larger drops that beat down upon his shaven head, he began to wonder where this path was leading him. Onwards he marched, now and again calling George's name despite his shouts being drowned by the wind whistling through the canopy. After approximately three hundred yards, he was met with a sheer drop ahead of him, opposite which was the small collection of houses and flats called The Junction. Kevin had his bearings once again: one of his short-lived jobs had been as a labourer during the construction of the estate. Suddenly he heard a familiar voice.

"Get away from me! Leave me alone!"

On Kevin's left, sat propped against a tree, was his friend George Williams. He was, like Kevin, soaked to the skin, but, more worryingly, his face was actually grey and he was clutching his chest with one hand whilst the other appeared to be fending off an unseen assailant. Kevin ran the few yards to George, looking for the cause of the old man's distress. Seeing nobody, Kevin grabbed George's free hand.

"George, it's me, Kev. What's up mate? You look like crap."

"Kevin? Is it really you?" George's voice was hoarse and he was clearly struggling for breath. "Get them away from me Kevin!"

"Get who away, mate? There's nobody here."

George's head moved left and right, his eyes wide, searching for the source of the voices that had terrified him.

"Kevin, I need help," he said. "A doctor, or ambulance. My chest feels like...it's agony."

Kevin didn't hesitate. Not having a mobile phone, he looked for the easiest way down the slope, then gently scooped George up in his beefy arms and carried him, baby like, back to the car. Placing him on the rear seat, lying down, he got back behind the wheel.

As he set off towards the hospital, Kevin asked who the youth was, and who had frightened George.

"I have no idea who the boy was. I've never seen him before." George paused. "As for the others, they were old friends.

"Dead friends."

Thursday 1145

"Emergency. Which service do you require?"

"Ambulance," said Steve, his eyes fixed on the form of his wife whose face was contorting with the pain of another contraction.

"Ambulance control room. Can I have your address please?"

Steve told the operator.

"What is the nature of the emergency?" continued the woman, exuding a professional calm that Steve considered somewhat incongruous.

"It's my wife. She's gone into labour. She's not due for a few weeks yet," replied Steve, successfully masking the concern in his voice, as much to reassure Katie as anything. There was a pause at the other end of the line.

"How many weeks early is she?"

"About three or four."

"Is it her first child?"

"No, it's our second. Why all the questions?"

Another pause. "Listen", said the woman, "we'll get somebody to you as soon as we can, but there's been a major pile-up on the motorway and we are having to prioritise any calls. It may be some time before we can get to you."

"What?" Steve's anxiety began to break through. "What am I supposed to do?"

"Your best bet is to phone your midwife. If she's not available... listen. Women have been having babies for thousands of years without needing hospitals. Your wife has done this once, so she knows what to do. Were you there? Remember, if the head comes first, there shouldn't be anything to worry about. If you have any problems, ring us back and we'll bump you up the list. Best of luck." She failed to mention the high infant mortality rate that ensued from more primitive birth conditions, but considered that a morale boost was the best that she could do in the circumstances.

Steve just stared at the phone for a moment after the operator ended the call.

"Well?" asked Katie. "How long will they be?"

Her husband turned and looked at her. "They aren't coming. At least, not yet." He paused for a second. "Have you got the midwife's number?"

Katie's face blanched. "On the pad...her name's Julie. Can you see it?" A hint of panic crept into her voice.

Steve found the number and dialled it. Explaining briefly, then listening for a moment, he said, simply, "Okay" and hung up. Turning to his wife, he looked her in the eye.

"She's tied up with a breech birth. We're on our own."

There was a moment's silence as they looked at each other. Katie was the first to speak.

"Oh, Steve, what are we going to do?" Her voice was beginning to break. "I need to push, but I can't do it on my own!"

"You're not on your own. We are in this together. We'll manage, somehow." He repeated the control room operator's speech about women giving birth in the past, but it had little effect on Katie. At that moment, her face was wracked with pain once more with the onset of another contraction. Waiting for it to subside, Steve took command of the situation.

"Joshie, we need to help Mummy." The little boy had been sat staring at his mother, incomprehension about to give way to anguish. At the sound of his father's voice, his face turned to Steve in anticipation.

"Joshie, I want you to go into the bathroom, and bring Daddy all the towels. Just one at a time. Can you do that for me?"

Without answering, the toddler clambered to his feet and left the room. As soon as he was out of sight, Steve gently helped Katie off the settee on to the floor. Reaching up her maternity dress, he pulled her knickers down her legs and off completely. Joshua returned with the first towel.

"Thanks, little man. Go and get me another one." To Katie he said "If you need to push, push with the next contraction. That's what they said last time, remember?"

His wife nodded briefly then gritted her teeth. A second later, she let out a scream of pain. Behind him, Joshua burst into tears. Steve looked between Katie's legs, and was immediately reassured by the sight of a mop of black hair.

"Katie, I can see the head!"

***

Janice Forsythe had been deep in thought during the journey from the hotel to the Melling's flat. She had sat in silence, wondering just what the future now held for her, but that changed when she spotted the figure of her father as Jack's car rounded the corner into Stricklands Lane.

"Jack! Look, it's my father. Where on Earth is he going? He'll catch his death in this weather!"

Jack diplomatically kept quiet: he hadn't told Janice about her father's illness. Furthermore, he had a good idea where Morgan was headed, but, again, decided that now wasn't the time to start telling ghost stories. That was the Mellings' job.

"I've got to get after him," she continued as Jack parked the car close to where they had seen Morgan. She opened the door of the Micra as soon as the car stopped and leapt out, heedless of the storm. Jack followed her, pausing only to lock the car before pulling his coat collar up and heading after her. Turning the corner where the stone abutment ended, Janice couldn't see any sign of her father. Jack guessed that Morgan had climbed up the embankment; looking up, he was rewarded with the sight of their quarry disappearing into the trees.

"Up there!" roared Jack, struggling to make himself heard above the wind. Together they struggled up the slope; Janice's boots were designed for fashion, not practicality and they slipped and slithered up the bank. Reaching the top, they looked around them but could see nobody.

"Where's he gone?" yelled Janice. Jack turned towards her but shook his head to indicate that he hadn't heard what she said. Janice moved closer to him.

"Can you see him?" shouted Janice through cupped hands.

Jack had a good look around before answering, then shook his head once more. They could see that Morgan could have gone one of two ways, and Jack was displaying uncharacteristic indecision as to which way to go first. Janice made his mind up for him.

"I'll go left," she bellowed, "you go right. I'll see you back here. He can't have got far."

Jack nodded his assent, despite feeling uncomfortable at leaving Janice alone up here. That youth had been up here previously, whoever he might be. Was he part of all this? Surely he couldn't be; he was too young to be caught up in a story that dated back more than sixty years. He turned to suggest that they stick together, but it was too late. Janice had set off and could be seen between the trees. Jack reasoned that the sooner he looked for the old man, the sooner they would be back together. Leaning into the wind, he set off along the right-hand curve of the former railway.

Morgan himself was transfixed with terror. The voices were louder still, though no more distinct. The youth stood to one side, and Morgan could see ahead of him a gap in the embankment where a small bridge had once stood. Now, a road to another housing estate, set in the triangle itself, passed through the gap some fifteen feet below.

Suddenly, the youth grabbed Morgan from behind, one arm around his chest and the other clamping a wet hand over his mouth. This is it, thought Morgan, my time is up. The realisation actually assuaged some of the fear as he resigned himself to whatever was planned for him. What he didn't expect was to be pulled behind one of the larger trees and held firm. A few seconds later, he saw why as his daughter appeared, running from the direction that he had come. Morgan struggled and tried to cry out, but the youth was far stronger and had no trouble keeping him still and quiet.

Janice was running and shouting at the same time: desperately looking for any sign of her father. The rain streamed down her face, getting into her eyes and blurring her vision. Too late, she saw the gap in the embankment, trying but failing to stop in time. The short heel of her boot caught in a crumbling joint between the bricks that had supported the bridge. Her momentum carried her over the edge, the drag from her stuck foot ensuring that she fell head first on to the road below.

Janice was not a heavy woman, but the force of landing on the back of her head from a height of fifteen feet was sufficient to wrench the fourth and fifth cervical vertebrae apart in a slicing motion that severed her spinal cord. Deprived of the electrical signals from her brain, her heart and respiration stopped immediately. In her last moments of consciousness, Janice Forsyth was confused, knowing that she must be hurt but wondering why she felt no pain. Then, with her brain starved of oxygen, darkness closed in. Her last mental image was of Paul, her dead husband, reaching out to her.

Thursday 1200

It is often said that when one life ends, another begins. So it was on that stormy Thursday. Katie Melling, screaming in unrelieved agony, had pushed with her contraction to deliver the head of her baby. Her husband, feeling the mental anguish of a man forced to witness his wife's pain whilst unable to do anything to alleviate it, gently supported the infant as it emerged. Her son, meanwhile, stood behind his father and cried for his mother.

"The head's out!" Steve said, unnecessarily. "Now, wait for the next contraction, and one more push should do it."

He sounded far more confident than he felt, wishing that either the midwife or an ambulance would appear. Not that he could actually let anybody in at that moment. Katie lay still, panting hard as she had been taught in her ante-natal classes, unable to influence events and thus placing her faith in her husband. Joshua's crying was distressing her, and she wasn't sure that she wanted him to witness at first hand the birth of his sibling. Catching her breath, she called to him.

"Joshie, come to Mummy. Come here, little man, and hold my hand."

Hearing his mother speaking rather than screaming partly mollified the little boy, and he edged past his father to take Katie's hand.

"Now, Joshie, in a minute Mummy is going to have to scream once more, but that will be the last time," she continued. "You hold my hand, and soon we'll have a new baby to look after."

Without speaking, Joshua sat next to his mother and put his little hand in hers. He was still sobbing, tears running down his nose and dripping off the end. The sight was enough to make Katie smile for the first time in a while. Moments later, she felt another contraction beginning.

"Time for Mummy to scream now, Joshie," she said, gently squeezing his fingers and beginning to pant once more. After a few seconds, she pushed once more, heedless of the agony as her birth canal was stretched by the shoulders of the baby. Simultaneously pushing and screaming, she suddenly felt her abdomen deflate.

Steve, grimacing once more at the sound of his wife's pain, was able to place his large hand under the baby and help it to emerge. It seemed to take an age for the shoulders to come into view but, as soon as he could actually touch the baby's body, he was surprised by the speed with which the baby came fully out of its mother, followed by what looked like at least a gallon of blood. For a few seconds, he just knelt there, staring at the scrap of humanity in his hands. Then, gathering his wits, he quickly wrapped the child in one of the towels that Joshua had brought from the bathroom and handed the bundle to his wife.

"Katie," he said excitedly as he placed the infant in her arms, "it's a girl. We have a daughter." Tears of joy were running down his face now as he placed a cushion under his wife's shoulders to help her to hold their newborn.

"Joshie, you've got a little sister," he continued as his son stared, dumbstruck, at the appearance of two blue eyes that slowly opened and seemed to look straight at him.

Steve realised that he had no idea what to do next, so he reluctantly left his wife's side to ring the midwife once more. Following her instructions, he tied off then cut the umbilical cord and waited for the placenta to appear. One more contraction, less painful this time, saw the final part of the birthing process complete, and Steve removed the messy remains to the kitchen so that, the midwife told him, it could be examined by a doctor when they finally got to hospital. When he returned to the living room, his daughter was suckling at her mother's breast.

Katie looked at him, a quizzical expression on her face. After a few seconds, she spoke.

"They've gone."

***

The grip around Cedric Morgan's face and body relaxed. Struggling free, he ran towards the edge and looked over. His daughter lay there, her hair splayed out around her; her eyes wide open but lifeless. Morgan was stunned: he stood, transfixed, as the reality finally dawned on him that his precious child was no more, snatched from him in a brutally trivial fashion. Almost simultaneously, the realisation that he was responsible for her demise made his knees buckle and he slowly collapsed to the ground.

Around him, unheard now, the ghostly figures stood murmuring. The stench of the sea was still present, but the atmosphere of hatred was much diminished, not that anything could penetrate Morgan's inconsolable grief. One figure, taller than the rest, appeared behind him and stood, silent. Sensing the presence, Morgan turned to look. The ghost of the signalman stared, unmoving, as if unsure what should happen next. The other figures moved behind him, drifting in and out of Morgan's peripheral vision. The voices, audible despite the gale, began once more.

We came to take him.

He cannot die in his sleep, safe in his own bed.

We have waited for this moment; take him!

But one voice, stronger than the others, took a different line.

He killed us, but he has killed his child too. It is better that he suffers that for his remaining days. Our day of reckoning will come, soon enough. Leave him be.

Morgan recognised the voice as that of his first victim and realised that, instead of his death being at the behest of the spectres, he was condemned to spend his last few weeks tormented by grief. His grandchildren were grown up now, but how would he explain their mother's death? Would he pass away hated by his own progeny? He had been willing to face up his fate a few minutes previously, but now the remains of his courage deserted him and he sat, watching the figures fade from view, bitter tears mingling with the rainwater that cascaded down his face.

Two hundred yards away, Jack Rimmer had come to the conclusion that he had taken the wrong path. He had tried, once or twice, calling Morgan's name but his voice was lost in the wind as it howled through the trees. His coat had given up trying to keep him dry, and he was now soaked to the skin. Wiping the rain from his eyes, he turned and retraced his steps.

It took him a few minutes to reach the point at which he and Janice had parted, and he was slightly perturbed that there was no sign of her there. Pausing for just a brief moment of indecision, he set off along the embankment that Janice had taken. Pushing through the trees, it took only a minute to reach the pathetic figure of their quarry, who was crying uncontrollably.

"Cedric, what's wrong?" asked Jack, suddenly very worried. "Where's Janice?"

Morgan just looked at him. It took a few seconds to compose himself sufficiently to speak.

"I'm so sorry, Rimmer," he gasped, between sobs. "She...she fell. I don't think that she could see where she was going...oh, Jack... she's dead. My girl is dead."

"What?" shouted Jack, incredulously. "Fell where? Are you sure that she's not just hurt?"

Morgan just gestured behind him, and Jack moved to the edge of the former bridge. Looking down, he could see two people crouched over somebody lying in the road. One looked up, saw Jack, and shook his head slowly. Jack, unbelieving, scrambled down the steep bank, unheeding of the remains of the wire fence that tore the sleeve of his coat and left a deep gash in his wrist. Running over to the people, a couple in their forties who had narrowly avoided running over Janice's body as they returned home, he caught sight of her face. Her skin was white, her eyes staring and devoid of life.

Jack was utterly bereft. Why now, he thought. Why her? For the first time, Jack had been in love, a feeling that he was sure was reciprocated, and she had been snatched from him by a cruel accident. Unable to stand up straight, Jack slumped against the bridge abutment as he struggled to make sense of the tragedy that had just torn his comfortable existence asunder. He started towards Janice's body, needing to hold her, just once, but the man held him back.

"You can't do anything for her. I've called the police; they'll be here in a minute."

The mention of the police brought Jack back to his senses to a degree. Realising that there would be some awkward questions to answer, Jack merely nodded, then told the man that Janice's father was still on the embankment and that he was going to fetch him.

As he turned round, he found himself face to face with the youth that he had seen from the window of the Melling's flat.

***

The first thing that Mike Simpson felt as he came round was neither the cold nor the wetness, although his lightweight jacket had offered scant protection against the wind and rain. Instead, he had witnessed the intense feeling of hatred rapidly diminish, finally disappearing along with the voices that had surrounded him as he passed out. Looking around him, he realised that he was not in the same place: the surroundings were similar but whereas before he had been surrounded by trees, now there was an open space to his right.

164

Turning his head that way, he could see an elderly man on his knees. He appeared to be crying, although with all the rain it was difficult to tell. A movement to his left caught his eye; by the time that he had looked in that direction all he could see was a tall figure with his back to Mike move into the trees and disappear. Mike was confused. How had he got there? Who was the old man? Climbing unsteadily to his feet, he moved towards the open space seeing for the first time the gap in the embankment. He walked over to the pathetic figure kneeling at the edge of the opening.

"Excuse me," he said. The man's reaction shocked him. The white haired man's head snapped round towards him and recoiled in terror.

"Get away from me!" he screeched. "You did this...you held me as she fell! She's dead, you know, and it's your fault!"

Mike backed away, alarmed by the man's violent reaction. Glancing over the edge, he could see some people on the road below, one of whom was lying close to the wall that held up the earthworks on which he stood. Thinking that he might get some more sense out of the people below, Mike followed the same path as Jack Rimmer had a minute earlier, although he was able to take his time and thus reach the bottom uninjured. As he reached the bottom, the nearest figure, another old man, turned and faced him.

"Who *are* you?" said the man abruptly, his face a mask of rage. Mike took a step back, his eyes wide with bewilderment.

"I...I'm Mike Simpson. What's going on?" The man took his arm and led him out of earshot of the people standing over Janice's body.

"Did you have anything to do with this?" said the man angrily, gesturing over his shoulder. Mike tried to look, but his view was blocked.

"No! Well, the truth is, I don't know. I just woke up, up there. That old man, he said it was my fault, but I don't know what he's talking about. Can you tell me?"

The man seemed to calm down a little, the anger on his face replaced by something different. His cheeks sagged and his head dropped a little. He thought for a moment, then spoke.

"You are a part of this, but what part I don't know. What I do know is that there is a dead woman over there, her father is the man you saw, and the police are on their way. On top of all that, there is no way they are going to believe what happened here."

"Why?" asked Mike. The answer actually gave him a crumb of comfort.

"Ghosts," said the man. "Do you believe in them?" he clearly wasn't expecting the answer that Mike gave him.

"I didn't, until they brought me here."

Thursday Evening

It had been a difficult few hours. The passer-by who had been at the scene of Janice's death was an off-duty policeman, hence his insistence on calling his colleagues. Fortunately, he had also witnessed the accident, and was able to make a statement to the effect that had not seen anybody near the woman that he had seen fall.

The police had interviewed Jack Rimmer, Cedric Morgan and Mike Simpson and released them pending the outcome of the coroner's inquest. Jack's story had seemed reasonable: it had, after all, been close to the truth. He told the police that he was researching the disappearance of his father and had discovered that Morgan had investigated the case at the time. Morgan, on the other hand (he said), felt responsible for Rimmer senior's death, and wanted to revisit the site before his own, imminent, demise. His daughter had accompanied them and, in the terrible weather, had become separated from them, leading to her tragic death.

Mike Simpson stuck to his excuse of researching old railways; the rather damp but still readable papers in his backpack appeared to support his story. The detective sergeant that interviewed all of them knew that there was something wrong, but had no credible explanation to back up his theory. He was especially puzzled as to why they should choose the worst day of the year, weather-wise, to visit the few visible remains of a railway that had been shut for over forty years.

Speaking to Cedric Morgan had been a waste of time. The man was inconsolable and unable to put a coherent sentence together. Thus the decision was taken to release all three men with stern warnings to make themselves available should the need arise, and to inform the police stations local to Janice's family to notify them of her demise. They were returned to Jack's car and, having tried unsuccessfully to speak to the Mellings, Jack had driven the three of them back to the hotel.

Now they sat around a single table in the adjacent pub having meant to have a meal but finding that none of them had an appetite. Instead they nursed large Scotches, which was a first for Mike but who had joined the others for fear of seeming ungrateful. Morgan stared morosely at his drink as Jack and Mike spoke about the day's events.

"You said that the ghosts brought you here," enquired Jack, his former career reasserting itself in spite of the grief that he felt over Janice. "Tell me about it."

Mike explained about the visitations, first at home, then at work, and described how he had been led to the site of the old railway. He spoke about how he had been in one place one moment, then had seemingly woken up somewhere different two hours later without being able to account for what had happened in between. He recounted his mother's story about his great-grandfather having been lost at sea and wondered aloud whether that had any bearing on the day's events. Jack made a mental note to research which ship he had been lost with, but thought that the SS Orestes would be a good place to start.

What neither man could work out was why Mike had been brought to Penwortham at all. There was a clear connection for both Jack Rimmer and Cedric Morgan, yet neither had been visited by the spirits. The Mellings had simply been living on the site of Jack's father's murder, hence their involvement, but why Mike? The only plausible (if any of this could be considered plausible) explanation was that the spectres were not physical manifestations and therefore needed a live person to do their dirty work. Simply taking over Morgan's body wouldn't have sufficed: they clearly wanted him to suffer. Well, they had succeeded in that, at least.

Jack realised that, with all this talk of ghosts, he had never actually witnessed anything supernatural. He recalled Steve Melling's comment, that this would make a great book. It dawned on him that there was a book in this, involving spooks, but not the paranormal kind. Jack leaned across to Morgan and spoke to him.

"Cedric, do you want to atone for what you have done?"

***

The Royal Preston hospital was experiencing a very busy day. In addition to twenty-four victims of the motorway pile-up, the emergency department had also seen the admission of one man in his eighties who had been carried into the waiting area in the arms of a burly, shaven-headed man. Both men were drenched, and Kevin Anderson's appearance caused the staff on duty to suspect at first that the old man's condition was the result of foul play. That impression lasted seconds: the triage nurse rapidly assessed George Williams' condition and he was quickly taken from Kevin to where a tired but competent doctor was able to make a formal diagnosis of myocardial infarction and get George on oxygen and transferred to the coronary care unit.

Kevin was left sitting in Accident and Emergency. Having given the staff George's name, address and the fact that he didn't think that he had any family, all he could do was sit and worry. Each time that the image of George's grey face looking at him, pleading, crossed his mind, Kevin found that his eyes filled with tears. Every few minutes, he would ask the receptionist on duty if there was any news: each time he was politely told that, when there was any news, he would be told. As he sat, fretting, another ambulance pulled up outside. Unable to restrain his curiosity, Kevin was surprised to see his drinking partner Steve Melling climb out, seemingly cradling a towel in his arms. He was followed by a woman who was helped into a wheelchair. Kevin was about to approach Steve when a woman's voice called to him.

"Mr Anderson, your friend is being moved to the ward. Would you like to go with him?"

Nodding his assent, Kevin followed the nurse who reunited him with George, now strapped to a trolley. His face was partially obscured by an oxygen mask, and a drip fed diamorphine and a thrombolytic into his left arm. Kevin, overwhelmed by the rather pathetic sight, wiped a tear from his eye and, on an impulse, held the old man's hand as a porter wheeled the trolley through the labyrinthine corridors and into the lift.

Steve Melling hadn't seen Kevin. His attention was fully occupied with his new-born daughter that lay sleeping in his arms. The ambulance had turned up after about ninety minutes, during which time Steve had become more and more concerned at Katie's lethargy and pallor. He knew that she had lost what looked like a great deal of blood, and the midwife's assurances that it was probably nothing out of the ordinary had worked for the first half hour; it hadn't occurred to him that, having fed the baby, his wife was simply exhausted. The fact that she had been sat in a pool of her own blood had done nothing to help her feel any better.

It had taken the staff on the neo-natal unit just a few minutes to ascertain that both mother and child were healthy and clean both up. The stub of the umbilical cord had been cut closer to the baby's navel; she had been put in a nappy and wrapped in blankets then placed in a clear Perspex cot next to her sleeping mother. Steve sat, Joshua on his knee, and looked at them both for a few minutes then took his son to a payphone to make two emotional telephone calls, first to his parents then to Katie's mother. He then returned to check on his wife and daughter, before taking Joshua to a small play area located close to the ward to await the arrival of the grandparents. As his son played, Steve allowed himself a satisfied grin. His expression went entirely unnoticed by the other new fathers nearby, all of whom had similar smiles on their faces, too.

***

"I want to write your biography," said Jack later that evening, his voice devoid of emotion. "Warts and all. I want you to tell me the truth about everything, good or bad, that you ever did, and I'm going to get it published."

Morgan thought for a moment, then nodded slowly.

"Very well," he replied, his voice soft, distant. "I suppose that at least some good will come out of this sorry affair, for you at least. There isn't long, you know, for me to tell you everything."

"Then we'd best get started. I'll drive you home tomorrow, then I'll have to go home myself. We'll start on Saturday morning."

Mike Simpson, whose eyes had been following the exchange as if watching a tennis match, was feeling somewhat left out.

"What is it that you did?" he enquired.

Seeing that Morgan was unwilling to speak to the young man, Jack replied for him.

"This man was recruited by MI5 from Oxford in the late thirties, and was with the service for fifty years. He has seen some history in the making, I can tell you."

"Not all his own doing, like this, I hope," said Mike.

"That's what I intend to find out. It'll take months to go through the records to check his story out, but I think that I possibly have my first best seller on my hands." A note of enthusiasm had crept into Jack's voice, a sentiment that lasted the split second that it took for the image of Janice, lying on the road, to once more explode into his thoughts.

The three of them were quiet for a minute or two, nobody knowing quite what to say next. A thought was forming in Mike's mind, but he wasn't sure that this was the right moment to raise the subject. Realising that the next day he would be on his way back to York and his humdrum existence, he spoke up.

"Jack, I...er...well, finding my way over here was really good." Lame, he thought. "What I mean is, my job doesn't take any thought, and going to the museum and everything to find this place it was, well, interesting." Not much better, Mike.

Both older men were looking at him now. He continued:

"I'm not saying this right, am I? Look, I managed to find this old railway all by myself, and I've never done anything like this before. The thing is, could I help you? Can I help with going through the records, or something?"

Jack pondered the lad's offer, but realised that he couldn't afford an assistant without a sizeable advance from a publisher, and that wasn't likely to be forthcoming in the timescale they had before them. He saw the disappointed look on Mike's face as he explained this, and felt bad for the boy. What happened next surprised both of them.

"I'll pay," interjected Morgan. "I'm not short of a bob or two, and I can't take it with me. I've caused you suffering too, lad, but hopefully you will be able to forgive me like Rimmer here probably can't. Just see that my grandchildren and their families get something out of it. What do you say, Rimmer?"

"Looks like you've got yourself a new job," said Jack, wondering how it might turn out.

Epilogue

To the true Communist, politics is their religion and the ultimate authority is the State. There is no room for God or an afterlife in such a philosophy, which is why George Williams spent the rest of his life in a state of confusion. His experience on the old railway embankment was clear evidence of an existence beyond the grave that contradicted his life-long beliefs.

His heart attack had been a moderate one, but which had left him permanently weak and unable to care for himself. He spent his last days in a nursing home, visited by Kevin Anderson from time to time, unable to make any sense of the events of that Thursday. He had been forced to sell his house to pay for his care, the proceeds of which had run out when he had his second, fatal heart attack. Only Kevin attended his funeral.

The flat on The Junction was too small for a family of four, so Steve and Katie Melling and their children began looking for a three-bedroom house not far away, and Steve landed a second job behind the same bar where he had met his wife. They invited Jack Rimmer to be Godfather and honorary grandfather to their daughter, whom they named Jacinta; an honour that Jack readily accepted.

Cedric Morgan succumbed to his cancer some nine weeks after the death of his daughter. Every day, for as long as he was coherent, Jack listened to his life story, recording the old man's words for transcription by Mike Simpson. After Morgan's death, the unlikely pair worked for nine months, cross-referencing Morgan's recollections with the official records, writing and re-writing each chapter until Jack was satisfied. He had been right about one thing: the book was a best seller. It was even serialised in a Sunday newspaper.

The hardest part of writing Morgan's biography had been the part about his daughter. Jack still dreamt about her; occasionally, when he allowed his mind to drift back to the day that she died, he could remember her unbuttoned blouse and the suggestive wink that had promised so much. That image was always followed by her lying in the road in the pouring rain, accompanied by a profound sense of loss that haunted him for years afterwards, accompanied by the guilt that he had had no such emotions for his lost father.

Mike Simpson had convinced his mother that his trip to Preston had been for a job interview: he claimed to have lied to her in case he hadn't been successful. He worked hard for Jack Rimmer, but when the book was complete he knew that he needed to follow a different direction. Inspired by long conversations with Jack, Mike applied for, and was accepted by, the Intelligence Corps of the Army. During basic training he discovered that he was not as proficient with a real rifle as the virtual one that had once occupied so many of his evenings, but also realised that he had a previously unknown talent for languages and quickly became fluent in Arabic. Like the Mellings, he never experienced anything supernatural again.

The old railway remained, silent, largely unnoticed and gradually reclaimed by nature. The people that had worked the line, like the line itself, faded into history. The ghosts were gone but, when the wind blew through the gaps in the embankments and between the trees, some would remark that the resulting moaning was almost human...

Author's Note

Much of the topography of this story is real. The West Lancashire Railway ran between Southport and Preston until 1964: a victim of the Beeching era. Preston was once a significant port; a substantial proportion of all wartime munitions shipments were from the Prince Albert Dock, and one visitor was indeed the SS Orestes. The small estate of flats and houses really exists on the site of Middleforth Junction, although under a different name. The characters are all entirely fictitious, as are all the events, all the product of an over-active imagination. And we all know that ghosts don't exist.

Don't we?